"I don't know what happened in there,"
Mac said tightly. "I saw it, but I don't
believe what I saw."

Ellie nodded and allowed him to open the door of the Corvette for her. She waited until they were driving away from the hangar before she spoke.

"Mac, what happened in there wasn't caused by anything physical. You're going to have to accept that sooner or later. Whatever is in that hangar is angry, and is carrying a lot of hatred."

"How do you know?"

"I felt it."

"This is crazy!"

"This thing isn't going to stop hurling tools at your people. Sooner or later, it could do some serious damage. Is that what you want, Mac? Do you want your people hurt? Maybe even killed?"

"This is just too much for me to believe, Ellie."

When she spoke again, her voice was a whisper. "I know it is...."

Dear Reader,

Welcome back to Shadows. It's hard to believe it's been a year since we first took you on a walk to the dark side of love, but it has been. And in honor of our first anniversary we have two very special books to entertain—and scare—you.

Lindsay McKenna is a name that needs no introduction, and we're thrilled to have her contributing to the line. *Hangar 13* is almost indescribable, mixing the truly terrifying threat of a restless spirit with the transcendent power of love. You'll hang on every word.

Lori Herter makes her full-length-novel debut with *The Willow File*. Is the past destined to repeat itself, even when repetition means tragedy? Or can the power of love overcome all obstacles and free two lovers from the curse of their ancestors' folly? Read this extraordinary book and the answers will be yours.

And in months to come, keep returning to Shadows to enjoy our unique mix of ingredients, the mix that chills you and thrills you, as our authors create memorable tales set in that mysterious region we call the dark side of love.

Enjoy!

Yours,

Leslie Wainger
Senior Editor and Editorial Coordinator

Please address questions and book requests to:
Reader Service
U.S.: P.O. Box 1325, Buffalo, NY 14269
Canadian: P.O. Box 1050, Niagara Falls, Ont. L2E 7G7

LINDSAY McKENNA

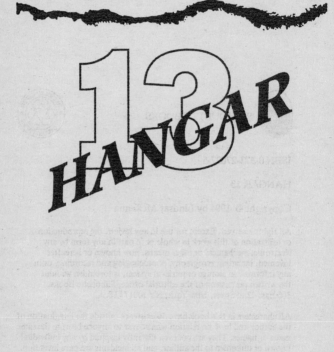

HANGAR 13

Published by Silhouette Books
America's Publisher of Contemporary Romance

SILHOUETTE BOOKS

ISBN 0-373-27027-5

HANGAR 13

Copyright © 1994 by Lindsay McKenna

This edition published by arrangement with Harlequin Enterprises B. V.

® and TM are trademarks of Harlequin Enterprises B. V., used under
license. Trademarks indicated with ® are registered in the United States
Patent and Trademark Office, the Canadian Trade Marks Office and in
other countries.

Printed in U.S.A.

Books by Lindsay McKenna

LINDSAY McKENNA

spent three years serving her country as a meteorologist in the U.S. Navy, so much of her knowledge comes from direct experience. In addition, she spends a great deal of time researching each book, whether it be at the Pentagon or at military bases, extensively interviewing key personnel.

Lindsay is also a pilot. She and her husband of fifteen years, both avid "rock hounds" and hikers, live in Arizona.

CHAPTER ONE

"Major Stanford, we've got trouble."

Mac Stanford looked up from the F-15 maintenance reports commanding his attention. Master Sergeant Gus Calhoon stood in his doorway, looking very unhappy. Placing his pen aside, Mac gestured for him to come in and shut the door.

"What is it, Gus?" Mac reared slowly back in his chair, the springs protesting. The sounds of his maintenance crew at work in the hangar filtered in through the open window.

Gus hovered hesitantly by the door. His oval face was badly wrinkled, his blue eyes flinty, his mouth pursed. Finally he came over to the desk. "Sir, it's happened again."

Mac's brow gathered in a frown. "Again? What's happened again?" He searched his mind for what Gus could be referring to. Not for the first time that morning, Mac wished he could be flying. It was 0900 hours, and the sky at Luke Air Force Base near Phoenix, Arizona was clear and just begging to be flown in. But a big part of his job was being maintenance commander for the squadron. The sky would have to wait.

"You know..." Gus pleaded in a low voice. He glanced toward the door as if to make sure it was shut.

Mac's dark brown brows dipped. "No, I *don't* know, Gus. Fill me in." He gestured toward his desk, which was littered with reports. "With the general inspection coming up, I'm lucky if I can remember my name." The inspector general's annual visit was a pain-in-the-neck event intended to determine the readiness of everything on the military base. Mac had a lot of pressures on him to get the squadron's planes in shape. If Luke got its usual high marks in the IG, he'd still be eligible for his "early" lieutenant-colonel leaves.

Rubbing his square jaw, Gus sat down in the leather chair in front of the desk. "Sir, remember two weeks ago when Sergeant Claris was in the cockpit of the F-15 and a wrench was thrown at her? It hit her in the back and she sustained some bruises and a laceration?"

Mac groaned. He placed his hands on the desk, scowling. "Yes . . . did you ever find out who threw it at her?"

Gus raised his eyes. "Sir, I didn't find anyone. Sergeant Claris was alone in Hangar 13, working late. There was no one around—just her."

"Well, what's happened now?" Mac tried to appear patient.

"It's Hangar 13 again. Only this time, it happened to Sergeant Burke. He was up on the scaffolding checking out an F-15 engine when he got nailed."

The master sergeant squirmed nervously in his chair. Mac was feeling a bit edgy himself, and his voice came out sharply. "Just tell me what happened."

"Yes, sir. Sergeant Burke was working on the wing, and his assistant, Sergeant Turner, was in the cockpit. This—this wrench came flying through the air and hit Burke on the head. It drew blood, sir, and damn near knocked him off the scaffolding."

Mouth twitching, Mac rose to his full six feet. "Who did it?"

"Uhh, no one . . . again, sir," Gus muttered.

Mac stared at him in disbelief. Gus Calhoon was a crusty thirty-year veteran of the air force and had seen it all, from Korea, to Vietnam and, of late, Desert Storm. There was no one more practical, more down-to-earth, than Gus. Flexing his fingers, Mac slowly came around the end of the desk and stood in front of him.

"Don't tell me—we've got a phantom wrench that flies through the air on its own?" Mac couldn't keep the sarcasm out of his voice. Gus wasn't the kind of person to make up stories like this. Maybe, at sixty, he was ready to retire. Mac was half his age, and he had a great respect for his master sergeant, who often performed near miracles with those gnarled, long fingers of his on the cantankerous F-15's in the hangar bay.

"I know, sir," Gus muttered apologetically, shooting him a sad look. "I can't explain how it happened, Major. But it did happen. Burke's over at the hospital getting stitches."

Mac heard the low, rumbling growl of two F-15's in the distance, and fought the impulse to take off for the air strip. "What about his crew? Could one of them have thrown it at him? Maybe as a joke?"

Sourly, Gus shook his head. He was dressed in the typical dark green fatigues that all maintenance people wore. Rubbing his hands slowly up and down his thighs, Gus said, "I questioned Burke's crew, and they swear they didn't even see it happen."

"What do you think? Could someone on Burke's crew be holding a grudge?"

"No, sir. He's well liked. You know that."

"I guess I do." Mac walked back around to his side of the desk. "This is the fourth incident in two months, Gus."

"Yes, sir, and the last two have caused injuries."

"Damn." Mac sat down in his chair and searched his master sergeant's grizzled features. "Okay, I'm open to suggestion. Its obvious you have something in mind. You've been holding it back ever since this stuff started happening. What is it?"

Gus stood up awkwardly, rubbing his hands on the sides of his fatigues in his characteristic gesture of nervousness. "Well, sir... I really hate to say it..."

With a wave of his hand, Mac muttered, "Nothing else you've offered explains these wrenches flying through the air. Try me."

"I really don't think you're ready for the explanation I have in mind, Major."

"Oh?"

"Sir, with all due respect, you're a cut-and-dried kind of officer, a no-nonsense sort of individual."

"All of that's true," Mac said, "but what does that have to do with your explanation?"

"Everything." Gus shook his head. "All right, sir, I'll tell you, but I don't want it held against me. Okay?"

Mac had always encouraged his people to speak their mind. He'd been maintenance officer for the squadron for three years, and the people who worked under his command were the best in the business, in Mac's opinion. One of his talents was to get the most out of them, and it had shown for three years in a row at IG time. Mac considered himself a good leader, and it was unusual for one of his people to consider him unapproachable. He said in a less-stern tone, "Whatever it is, Gus, I'll handle it. Just sit down and tell me."

The tone worked miracles on Gus, who instantly brightened. Rubbing his hands against his thighs, he sat down and said, "About two months ago my wife, Shelly, went to a metaphysical workshop put on by this woman named Ellie O'Gentry." He shrugged a little apologetically to Mac. "Shelly has always been interested in psychic stuff. Anyway, she came home bubbling all over the place about this Eastern Cherokee shamaness and how she'd helped change Shelly's outlook on life. I didn't give it a thought—then. But—" Gus cleared his throat "—I do now."

"What's this got to do with our problem?" Mac demanded.

"Well, sir, after the second wrench was thrown at someone over in Hangar 13, I told Shelly about it. She said that this woman, Ellie, had talked about a phenomena called discarnate souls, spirits who were 'stuck' in a certain place. She said these spirits some-

times did things to get a human being's attention."
Gus gulped and looked at Mac, waiting for some kind
of reaction. When there was none, he went on hastily.
"This shamaness was taught soul recovery and extraction by her mother, a medicine woman who still
lives on the reservation back in Cherokee, North Carolina." With a wave of his hand, Gus said, "Now, I
don't believe in all that stuff. I'm a prove-it-to-me
man, sir. But I've seen such positive changes in my
wife since she went for a healing, I've got to believe *she*
believes something happened. Anyway, one of the
things Ellie O'Gentry does is communicate with spirits." Gus looked over his shoulder toward the door. "I
don't know, Major. Maybe we've got an unhappy
spirit of some sort out there in Hangar 13."

Mac sat there absorbing Gus's explanation. His
master sergeant, obviously embarrassed to bring up
the subject, had colored a bright red. A huge part of
Mac wanted to laugh, but he swallowed the urge in
light of Gus's sincerity. With a sigh, he said, "That's
a bit farfetched, isn't it, Gus?"

"Yes, sir, I know it is. But—" he rolled his eyes "—I
honestly don't have a better explanation why wrenches
are suddenly flying through the air."

"Dammit." Mac got up and began to pace the
length of his small, cramped office. Books on F-15 jet
maintenance covered two walls of his office; a desk,
chair and filing cabinet were squeezed into the narrow space. Mac walked over to the coffeemaker and
filled two cups with the strong brew. He handed one
to his master sergeant.

"Thank you, sir."

Mac eased his frame against the desk as he sipped his steaming black coffee. "I think we need to deal with facts, and facts only, Gus."

"No disagreement from me on that, sir." Gus took a gulp of coffee and then rested it against his thigh. "These are the facts—four wrenches have been thrown at our people. In three out of the four cases, the people were working alone, in Hangar 13, late at night. The fourth incident took place with other people around, but they swear they didn't throw the wrench."

"Could any of these be hoaxes?"

Gus shrugged. "These are our top people, Major. They're happy doing what they're doing, none of them have any personal problems and they're all up for either reenlistment or another rating."

Mac knew his people were happy with him, and with the job they were doing in the air force. Scratching his head, he muttered, "It just doesn't fit. I can't see any of our personnel over in 13 causing that kind of trouble. They're the cream of the crop."

"I know," Gus said. "Not only that, none of them willingly came forward to tell me about it. In each case, someone from the crew learned about it second-hand and came and told me."

Sipping his coffee, Mac thought long and hard for a moment. He slanted a glance at Gus. "This spirit theory is the worst."

Gus grinned a little. "Yes, sir, I know it is."

"Hangar 13 was built two months ago, and a week after we moved in, this wrench-throwing started."

"Yes, sir... I dunno, maybe it's the number 13. You know how unlucky it is."

Mac snorted. "I don't believe in that malarkey one bit, Gus."

"Yes, sir. It was just a thought...."

Frustrated, Mac turned and walked around the desk. He set the coffee mug down a little sharply. "My career would be washed up if I told my commanding officer I was checking out this shamaness because our people were getting nailed with flying wrenches."

"I know," Gus muttered unhappily. "That's why I really hesitated telling you about her."

"Is this woman a nut case?"

"Sir?"

"You know," Mac growled, "one of those New Age types?"

"Uhh, I don't know, sir. Shelly knows more about her. I never met the woman. I've only heard about what she does.

"I guess the only other thing we could do is call in the Air Police to start an investigation," Gus offered unenthusiastically after a moment.

"No way." The last thing Mac needed in his command was an ongoing investigation. He knew it would upset the rhythm he'd established on base if the Air Police started nosing around. And right now, with the IG two months away, he wanted to keep his people happy and on an even keel.

"Well," Gus hedged carefully, "I guess it wouldn't hurt any to talk to this lady, would it? Maybe she could shed some light on what's going on."

Fuming, Mac sat down. "Gus, this conversation doesn't leave this office. Understand?"

Gus straightened in the chair to almost an at-attention stance. "Yes, sir! Not a word of it, Major."

"Fine," Mac muttered. "Call your wife and get the address and phone number of this woman." He stared hard across the desk at his master sergeant. "I don't like this, Gus."

"I understand, sir." Gus rose quickly. "But we're at a point where we're running low on options. I'll get the info and have it on your desk within the hour, sir."

"Fine. Dismissed."

"Yes, sir."

Mac sat in his office for a long time, the noise from Hangar 13 activities vaguely lapping into his awareness. The blue sky still beckoned like a lover calling him, and now he had to deal with this on top of all his other problems. He sighed in frustration as he eyed all the maintenance reports still awaiting his signature. With so many bases and stations being closed, Luke was getting extra squadrons, and more hangars were being built to accommodate the heavy influx of fighters and pilot personnel. Hangars 13, 14 and 15 had recently been completed, and construction was still underway on three more. The paperwork showed no signs of abating.

Flying had always helped Mac solve the multitude of problems he handled on a daily basis. He wanted to leave his office, hitch on a pair of g-chaps and grab his helmet from the squadron locker. But it seemed that, for today at least, he was grounded.

Tonight, he'd check out this Ellie O'Gentry on his way home. He'd have to be careful, though—he couldn't let his bosses find out he was chasing this kind of lead. He decided to change out of his air force uniform and get into some civvies before he went to see her. That way, if he didn't like her, she'd never know who he was or why he'd come. Mac couldn't take any chances—if his superiors ever learned about this, he'd lose his chance for an early promotion. Hell, they'd probably drum him right out of the air force.

Ellie O'Gentry was kneeling in the backyard at her small Santa Fe-style house, tending her garden. At six p.m. the May sunlight had gone westward, and the temperature had cooled down enough for her to get some work done. She was dressed casually in jeans and a short-sleeved, mint green blouse, minus her usual sandals—Ellie always went barefoot when weeding. Her long, black hair was tamed into one thick braid down the center of her back, tendrils clinging damply to her brow and temples as she worked.

Sinking her long fingers into the warm, fertile earth, she smiled to herself. Gardening gave her such a grounded feeling; it always seemed to bring her closer to the natural energy of Mother Earth. Using the trowel, she dug around each of her carefully tended tomato plants. The song that she'd been humming, a sweat-lodge song used for healing, spilled softly from her lips. It was a song her mother had taught her, a lullaby used to help the seriously ill gather hope and strength to heal.

Ellie stopped humming abruptly and looked up. Had she heard something? She wasn't sure. She sat up, her dirt-encrusted hands coming to rest on the thighs of her jeans. What had snagged her peripheral attention?

She quickly switched to her more intuitive side, a subtle transfer of attention through another lens of her being, and tilted her head. No, the sound she'd heard hadn't been verbal. Her gaze riveted on the corner of the house that led to the front door. Someone was coming. She could sense him—and he was a male. Who? Brushing some of the dirt from her hands, Ellie was perplexed. She didn't have any appointments scheduled for today.

Before she could muse further, she saw a man—a scowling man—very quietly turn the corner of the house. He halted and stared at her, his scowl deepening. Automatically, she scanned him with her intuitive "eyes," a kind of sixth sense that allowed her to see inside her unexpected visitor.

Instantly, Ellie got in touch with the stranger's tenseness. He was wary. And frustrated. With whom? Her? She certainly had never seen this man before. If she had, she would never have forgotten him—he made too vivid an impression. She sensed nothing dangerous about him, so she switched back to her visual eyes and took a good long look at him. He was tall and wiry, reminding her of a cougar she'd seen from time to time while she was growing up in the Great Smoky Mountains of North Carolina. His hazel eyes were large and intelligent looking, though shadowed. He had a square face, with a stubborn-looking chin. His dark brown hair was very short and neatly cut. He was handsome in a rugged kind of way. Ellie liked the crinkles at the corners of his eyes; they suggested he smiled a great deal. But he wasn't smiling now, and his hands were draped tensely across the hips of the tan chino pants he was wearing.

He had a decided charisma, and Ellie found herself drawn very powerfully to the man. Was it his proud posture, his broad shoulders thrown back with confidence? The look of the eagle in his eyes, which told her he missed very little? Or something else? He seemed as if he were a warrior of some kind, a fighter, or someone who enjoyed challenging life in some way. There were a lot of angles to the man—sharp edges, perhaps, she mused, as she slowly got to her feet.

As Ellie approached him, she could feel his perusal, direct, intense and assessing. A part of her wanted to throw up a wall of defense, to guard herself against his almost-violating look, but something told her she didn't have to.

For an instant, she felt the man's surprise, and then, on its heels, his heat and desire. Desire? None of her impressions made any sense to her. The surprise lingered in his eyes, and she wondered what he wanted from her. Perhaps he was lost and looking for directions.

"Can I help you?" Ellie asked.

Mac tried to cover his surprise. The barefoot woman walking toward him was nothing like what he had expected. She was in her late twenties, he guessed; her gold-colored skin accentuated the oval face and high cheekbones typical of Native Americans. Strands of her thick black hair were loose around her hairline, some tendrils sticking to her brow and temples, emphasizing her earthy beauty. Could this woman be the shamaness? She looked so. . . normal.

Her gaze was direct, inquiring, and Mac felt her confidence and strength. She walked with a sureness, a serene kind of balance that was undeniable. He allowed his hands to fall from his hips.

"Yes, I was looking for a Ms. Ellie O'Gentry."

Ellie halted a good six feet away from him. "That's me. Who are you?"

"I'm Mac Stanford."

"Are you lost, Mr. Stanford?"

"Excuse me?"

Ellie watched the play of surprise and hesitation in his eyes. "Are you lost?"

His mouth pulled into a grin. "No."

She liked his eyes. They were a mixture of green, gold and brown, reminding her of the green trees, the fertile brown earth and the gold of Father Sun. And when the corners of his mouth drew hesitantly into a brief smile, she felt an incredible blanket of warmth surround her. The feeling caught Ellie off guard.

Mac pulled a piece of paper from his shirt pocket. He'd worn a conservative blue-and-white striped shirt and comfortable jogging shoes. "Your name was given to me by Mrs. Shelly Calhoon."

"Oh...yes." Ellie held his interested gaze. "You're here regarding soul recovery and extraction?"

"Excuse me?"

It was her turn to smile. "I'm making assumptions, Mr. Stanford. Why are you here? You don't have an appointment. At this time of day, I reserve my time for my garden."

"I see. . . ." Mac scrambled for a reply, because he knew she was going to ask him to make an appointment and leave. There was something fascinating about Ellie O'Gentry. She was decidedly Native American in appearance—so why was her last name O'Gentry? All of a sudden, Mac had a lot of questions that had nothing to do with his original reason for coming.

"Look," he murmured apologetically, "I'm sorry for not calling first. But . . . something's come up and your name was given to me. If I could just have about fifteen minutes of your time?"

Rubbing the last of the drying soil off her hands, Ellie asked, "Then you're a friend of Shelly's?"

"In a roundabout way," Mac hedged. He watched as she leaned down to the faucet and rinsed her hands. Ellie's movements were sure and graceful. It wasn't often he met a woman with so much confidence. Whatever life had dealt Ellie, she'd come out stronger for it.

Ellie straightened and dried her hands on her jeans. "Why do I get the feeling you're not who you seem to be?"

Heat nettled Mac's cheeks, and he realized with a start that he was blushing. Unsettled, he said, "I'm looking for a psychic, somebody who can help answer a question I have."

"I'm a shamaness, Mr. Stanford, not a psychic. There's a difference."

"There is?"

Ellie held on to her patience. He was genuinely surprised, and she could feel his intense need to talk with her. "A big difference. I was just going to make dinner—"

"I'm sorry, I didn't mean to interrupt your dinnertime—"

"No, that's okay. Why don't you come in for a cup of coffee and you can tell me why you're here and what you want from me."

Mac nodded and followed her around to the front door. Ellie seemed to have an unsettling ability to see right through him. Or was that just his imagination? He snorted to himself and followed her into the cool confines of the stucco home.

The living room was well lit; the floor, a warm, golden pine, was covered with a Navajo rug of gray, white and black. Above the ivory couch hung an Indian flute adorned with several long brown-and-white feathers. There were also several framed pictures of flowers and pastoral landscapes.

The ivory-colored walls made the most of the light, and Mac liked the large array of greenery displayed on both sides of the large picture window. Ellie had brought the outdoors in; she clearly loved the land.

Mac followed her across the living room and into the pale yellow kitchen. She gestured to a glass table and the bamboo chairs that surrounded it.

"Why don't you have a seat, Mr. Stanford, and I'll be back in a moment." She pointed to her jeans. "I'm dirty."

He nodded and eased one of the bamboo chairs away from the table. "Sure, go ahead." Good, this would give him a chance to check her out further. Mac felt a little guilty about his deception, because Ellie seemed honest, straightforward and generous with her time—considering he didn't have an appointment.

What did a shamaness do? He'd wondered that all the way over here. He didn't have a clue and didn't want to guess. Soul recovery and extraction? It sounded like a visit to the dentist's office! Smiling, he walked over to the kitchen counter. There were four ceramic canisters, each painted with flowers, making the counter look as if it was in bloom, too. Small pots of cactus sat on the windowsill above the sink.

Looking around the kitchen, Mac decided that Ellie's home didn't look particularly out of the ordinary. Sitting down, he heard soft, Native American flute music emanating from another part of the house. Somehow, the picture he had of Ellie just didn't jibe with what he was observing. Tapping his fingers absently on the clean glass surface of the table, Mac noticed the fresh bouquet of wildflowers, some red, some pink and others yellow. He smiled. How long had it been since he'd seen wildflowers? He decided that Ellie was the exact opposite of him: he was a man who owned the sky and loved to live in it. She was a woman of the earth, firmly planted in it, bare feet and all.

"Would you like some coffee?"

Mac jumped. Ellie had entered so quietly he hadn't heard her. She was still in her bare feet, although now she wore a lightweight denim skirt that grazed her ankles and a fresh, white blouse. Her hair had been brushed, too, the blue-black locks caught up in a loose ponytail with a bright red scarf.

"Yes . . . please."

Ellie went to the sink and began to prepare her coffeepot, an old-style one that perked on the electric stove. "So what brings you here, Mr. Stanford?" She turned to him briefly and saw that his darkly tanned face was still tense, his eyes still shadowed.

"Well, I've got a problem, and you were suggested as a person who might be able to help me."

Ellie put the coffee grounds into the basket, put the lid on the pot and placed it on the stove. She got down two cups and set them on the table. Going to the refrigerator, she took out the cream. She sat down and placed the creamer between them on the table. "What problem?" she asked.

Mac cleared his throat. "I'm a little embarrassed to even talk about it, to tell you the truth."

"Why?" Ellie folded her hands and rested her chin against them. Mac Stanford was blushing again. His cheeks were a dull red color, and she could almost take pity on him—almost, but not quite. He was hiding something from her, and that made her wary. Still, she had to fight a powerful attraction to him. His self-confidence was like sunlight, something that she honored in any person, but his was charismatic—and dangerous—to her.

With a shrug, Mac said, "Normally, I don't go to a psychic—"

"Excuse me, but I think we need to get our terminology straightened out before we go any further."

Mac stared at her. "Okay."

"I'm a shamaness, Mr. Stanford."

"Isn't that the same thing?"

"Yes and no. First of all, I'm a healer." Ellie opened her long, spare hands toward him. "I'm half Eastern Cherokee and half white. I was born and raised on the Cherokee reservation in North Carolina. My mother is a medicine woman for our people, and so is my sister, Diana. I inherited some of my mother's metaphysical abilities, but they are expressed differently through me than through her or my sister."

"Metaphysical?" Mac felt like a first grader.

"Meta means 'beyond the physical or seen world.'" Ellie pointed to her eyes. "When something is *meta*physical, it means that it's beyond our visual capability." A slight smile touched her mouth as she pointed to the center of her forehead. "But we all have another 'eye' we can see with. This third eye is called the brow chakra. Most people don't use it. They're only in tune with the left side of their brain, the side that uses their physical eyes to view the three-dimensional world. But the right brain, the intuitive side, has an eye, too, of sorts. It's located here, in the center of our forehead."

"Hold it," Mac said, raising his hands. "You've lost me completely."

"I don't really get the feeling you want to know anyway, Mr. Stanford," Ellie said patiently.

Mac sat back, frowning. Her directness was unsettling to him. Or, maybe more to the point, he wasn't used to finding this typically male trait in a woman. "You're right," he admitted.

"So," Ellie said, folding her hands and challenging him with her gaze, "why don't you tell me the real reason you're here? Are you a police detective? An undercover agent?"

CHAPTER TWO

For the third time, Mac felt heat in his cheeks. How long had it been since he'd blushed? A long time. Maybe before he and Johanna had gotten married. He pushed that painful thought aside. Mac knew he had to be honest with Ellie.

"It's nothing like that, Ms. O'Gentry." He frowned and then met her direct, intelligent gaze. Her eyes were a golden brown color, reminding him of sunlight dancing off the surface of water. If Mac didn't know better, he'd think she was smiling at his predicament. At first, a bit of anger stirred in him, but then he realized it was his own fault that he'd placed himself in this embarrassing position.

"I'm a major in the air force. I fly F-15's," he said. "I'm also the maintenance officer for our squadron." Almost instantly, Mac saw Ellie relax.

"That's a good start, Major Stanford," Ellie said. "Go on." She smiled slightly, because she saw how terribly uncomfortable he was with her—or, more precisely, with what she symbolized. Still, she liked Stanford's ability to be honest when he was challenged, and that was commendable.

Mac took a deep breath and dove into the story of the flying wrenches in Hangar 13. Ellie sat quietly, without interrupting, while he stumbled through a detailed explanation of the four incidents. She just wasn't what he'd expected. Mac wasn't sure *what* he'd expected, but certainly not this quiet, introspective, intelligent woman whose beauty was more than skin-deep. His gaze kept drifting from her beautiful eyes, framed with thick, black lashes, to her soft mouth. He found it difficult to concentrate on the story when he really wanted to study her instead.

So he divided his attention. He had always been good at that, and Johanna had resented it. She had always accused him of only half listening to her and had said she could sense that his mind was elsewhere. And it was true, Mac acknowledged. But he couldn't help it—it was part of his nature, part of what made him such a good fighter pilot. His eyes might be on the instruments or on the terrain outside the cockpit canopy, but his hearing was elsewhere, and his physical body was subconsciously recording sensations, too. Mac had tried repeatedly to explain this to Johanna, but she never understood. Or perhaps she had, and just hadn't been able to accept it.

Ellie was listening with her ears, but she had allowed her senses to blossom fully and take in the complete spectrum of Mac Stanford. She liked that fact that he talked with his hands, that he was animated about the story he was sharing with her. Still, she could see that part of his attention was diverted toward studying her face, and that his interest was on more than just a professional level. Smiling to herself, she admitted that she was just a little interested in Mac Stanford on a personal level, too.

"So," Mac said, "that's the story."

Ellie nodded. "And you're looking for an explanation for this phenomena, Major?"

"I guess I am. I really don't know."

"What you're really saying is that you don't believe it could happen in the first place. That the phenomena has to have a human culprit behind it, not a ghostly one."

"Are you always this direct?"

Ellie grinned. "It pays to be honest, don't you think, Major?" She saw the amusement come to his hazel eyes and his mouth curve upward briefly. When Mac Stanford smiled, she felt the sunlight of his energy surround her like a warm, soft blanket.

"Yes." Mac struggled inwardly for a moment. "I guess I'm not used to such directness in a woman like yourself."

"Really?" Ellie tilted her head, her hands resting against her chin. "What did you expect?"

Uncomfortable, Mac muttered, "I had this picture in my head of an old woman in a gypsy outfit sitting over her crystal ball."

Ellie laughed. It was a full laugh, rich yet soft.

Mac stared at her as she leaned back in the chair, tilted her head back and allowed the wonderful laughter to escape. In that moment, surrounded by her laughter, he felt an incredible need to know her better—as a woman.

"I can surmise two things about you, Major," Ellie said, placing her hands on the table and engaging his stare. "First, you don't believe in what I do any more than you believe the moon is made of green cheese. Secondly, you're a prove-it-to-me kind of man, totally stuck in his left brain. I'll bet you dismiss any intuitive thoughts if you can't prove, weigh or see results. Am I right?"

"I believe what my eyes see," Mac said, a bit defensively.

"And I don't. We're poles apart, Major. I live in worlds that you don't believe exist."

"Well—" Mac cleared his throat "—I don't think that matters in this case. I came to you asking for an explanation. It doesn't have to be one I believe in."

"Perhaps," Ellie said softly.

"I'm here. I think that proves *something*."

"Maybe," she agreed.

Getting a bit frustrated, Mac said, "Tell me what you charge and I'll pay you for the information."

She got up, went over to the refrigerator and drew out some vegetables. Twisting to look over her shoulder, she said, "There is no charge, Major."

"Why not?"

"If I can answer your questions without going into a shamanic-journeying state to do it, I will. I never charge in this kind of a situation." She began tearing lettuce into small pieces over a large ceramic bowl.

"I don't know what to make of you."

Ellie smiled and began cutting up a carrot. "At least you're honest. That's a good place to start, Major." Her ex-husband, Brian, had pretended to be interested in what she did, but it had all been a grand lie for his grand plan. All he really wanted was a companion in bed—and a housekeeper. It soon became clear that Brian didn't believe in her world, but Ellie had tried to make things work, hoping they could find some kind of common ground. Finally, after three years of Brian's continuing abuse over her beliefs, she'd had to get out.

"I may not like the truth, Ms. O'Gentry, but it's better than the alternative."

Her smile broadened. "That is one thing we agree on completely, Major."

"Call me Mac, will you?"

"Okay. You can call me Ellie if you want." She sensed his defensive walls slowly dissolving, and that was good. As he sat sipping the coffee, she could see the questions in his eyes.

"I'm caught between a rock and a hard place," Mac admitted. In a bittersweet way, he enjoyed watching Ellie prepare the salad. It reminded him of his broken marriage, of a happier time in his life. Mac missed the hominess that marriage had provided him.

But Ellie was nothing like Johanna. She wasn't modellike as Johanna had been, but reminded Mac of a woman in a Titian painting—ample, curved and rounded in all the right places. Ellie reminded him of a true earth mother.

She placed the salad on the table between them. "Why don't you get up and set the table, since you're staying for dinner?"

Mildly shocked, Mac got up. He saw her eyes dancing with laughter.

"Are you stunned because you're staying for dinner or because I'm asking you to help out?"

He smiled a little sheepishly as he moved to the cupboard that Ellie pointed to. "Both."

"You don't wear a wedding ring, but you behave like you've been married. Are you divorced?"

Struck by Ellie's insights, Mac opened the cupboard and took down two white ceramic plates. "*Are* you psychic?"

Laughing, Ellie shook her head. "No, just a watcher of people in general. I saw this look of longing on your face, and noticed you had no wedding ring on your finger. I figured you were probably divorced and missing the good life that marriage provides."

"Guilty," Mac murmured, placing the plates on the table. "I'm divorced, and you're right—I miss married life."

"All of it or some of it?" she challenged.

Mac placed flatware at each plate. "Why do I get the impression you're a feminist?"

"Because where I come from, there is none of this 'man rules the roost.' My people are matriarchal, and that means women are held in just as high esteem as any man. We own the land, and it's passed on from one woman to another, instead of from man to man."

"Reverse of what it is out in the real world."

"Oh?" Ellie whispered. "My world is just as valid as yours, Major."

"Touché." Mac smiled a little and sat back down.

"You're not done yet, Major."

"I'm going to earn this dinner, I can tell."

"And then some." Ellie pointed to the top of the refrigerator. "Get a couple of those rolls and bring them down. Put them in the microwave, please."

Ordinarily, Mac might have been annoyed, but he wasn't. Ellie intrigued him. He liked her use of authority and the way she made him a part of the kitchen—whether he felt he should be helping or not. Johanna had always shooed him out of the kitchen and called him when dinner was ready. Retrieving the rolls, he placed them in the microwave. Then he took a butter dish from the refrigerator and set it on the table.

"Very good," Ellie praised with a laugh as she put hamburger meat into the skillet she'd heated. "You're getting the idea."

"Is this called karma?" he teased as he stood next to her, leaning against the kitchen counter, his hands resting on it.

Ellie nodded. "Our whole life is karma as far as I'm concerned. The people we meet, the ones we work with, the ones we bump into on the street." She glanced up at his face, which now seemed more relaxed. "Karma is about living life, Major."

"Mac."

"Yes..."

"I feel like I've stepped into a whole new world here."

"You have. I'm Native American, raised to respect all people as equal. I'm a shamaness, and I've been trained to look at reality very differently than you."

"I'm a city kid from Portland, Oregon," Mac admitted. "My father was an electrical engineer until he died of a heart attack at forty-five. My mother stayed at home and raised me and kept house."

"And I'll bet she never went out and had a job or a life other than that."

"Correct."

"You white men are a spoiled bunch," Ellie said with a chuckle. "One hamburger or two?"

"Two, please."

"Manners. That counts with me."

"Are you always this feisty or is this something special for me?"

"I'm not treating you any differently than I would anyone else—regardless of gender." Ellie turned the hamburgers in the skillet. "Get the mustard and ketchup from the refrigerator?"

"Sure." Mac opened the refrigerator door.

"How long have you been divorced?"

Mac hesitated as he placed the ketchup on the table. "Two years."

"You don't seem to be over it yet."

Her insight was unsettling. He paused briefly, then said, "I think if you love someone, it's tough to leave it behind."

"The heart never forgets," Ellie agreed gently, handing him his burgers. "All our good and bad memories are held in it. Come on, let's eat. I'm starving."

Mac ate with relish. The baked beans, hamburgers and garden salad were perfect. It had been a long time since he'd had a home-cooked meal. Ellie had a healthy appetite, too, unlike Johanna, who had weighed every ounce of food she ate, always scared of gaining a few pounds. Ellie certainly wasn't fat, but Mac saw that she truly enjoyed her food and obviously didn't agonize over caloric content.

"Do you have any grounding in metaphysics, Mac?"

He shook his head. "Absolutely none."

"With your engineering background, the only thing you know is your left-brain reality."

"Is that a compliment or an insult?" Mac liked the smile she gave him as she wiped her fingers on her pink cloth napkin.

"Neither. It's merely an observation." Ellie pointed to the right side of her head. "I need to give you some basic information so you'll understand what is potentially happening in your Hangar 13."

Mac added more ketchup to his second hamburger. "Okay, shoot."

"Native Americans and women tend to be right-brain dominant. Science has established that the right brain's function is very different from the left brain's. The left hemisphere processes information based on logic, on physical evidence from our senses. It can speak to us with a sound, a voice, and we all hear it." She tapped the right side of her head. "The right brain can't speak to us in the same way."

"So," Mac said, buttering a second roll, "does the right brain 'talk' to us?"

"Excellent question," Ellie praised. "Yes, it does, but in a far-more-subtle form. You'd call it intuition, or a gut feeling. I'm sure you've heard talk of women's intuition. Well, some women are simply more in touch with their right brain. Unfortunately, society doesn't always take this kind of knowledge seriously."

"I see."

"You may 'see,' in one way, Mac, but you can't really understand the process. In the Native American culture, we are taught that women know what they know, and that it is different from how men know the same thing. One way isn't more right than another."

"Johanna, my ex-wife, used to tell me that when she was in college, she'd come up with the right answers on her math tests, but she wouldn't be able to remember the formula or how she got the answer."

Ellie smiled broadly. "That's right. That's the right-brain way—making the quantum leap to the answer. It doesn't care how it got the answer like the left brain does."

"She flunked the algebra course because she couldn't prove how she arrived at the answers."

"I'm sure she did, because most schools and colleges are based on left-brain thinking."

"How did you do in school?"

"I was able to stay home and be taught by my mother. Right-brain methods of learning are very different from left-brain methods. My mother used a very practical teaching method with me—show-and-tell. I learned by doing, or what is known as hands-on experience. My father, who is a white man and a plumber by profession, taught me his business as I grew up. I watched him do it, and then mimicked his actions. It was very practical."

"Not a lot of theory, philosophy or left-brain stuff?"

"Precisely." Ellie got up and removed their plates. "Would you like a slice of homemade cherry pie?"

Mac grinned sheepishly. "Will I be indicted if I say yes?"

"There's no guesswork with you," Ellie said with a chuckle as she removed the cherry pie from a cupboard and cut two thick slices.

"My stomach has always been my downfall," he admitted. "I like home cooking. There's nothing wrong with that."

"There's nothing wrong with it as long as you help with the cooking and not just the eating." She smiled and put the plate before him.

"I can't even boil water. I'd make a crummy cook. Thanks, this looks good."

"That's because your mother never made you come into the kitchen and learn to cook." Ellie sat down and enjoyed the silence that blanketed them while they ate dessert. It was obvious Major Mac Stanford had enjoyed the meal.

"Do you make your own meals?" she wondered aloud.

With a shrug, Mac said, "Usually I go to a restaurant off base for dinner."

"I see...."

"I'm sure you do." He liked the sparkle in Ellie's eyes as he met and held her gaze.

"Let me take it a step further, then. The right brain, scientifically speaking, is the creative side of ourselves. It is the seat of our emotions, our feelings. The left brain is tied into lists, black-and-white issues, practicality and strict visual observation."

"That's why women are more emotional than men?"

"I'm not letting you get away with that generality," Ellie said grimly. "Let's put the shoe on the other foot, Mac—both genders have both brain hemispheres in their head. There is nothing that says men can't begin utilizing their right brain more."

With a groan, Mac said, "Now I get it. This is the sensitive man of the nineties you're talking about, the one who is using his right brain?"

"*And* his left." Ellie waved her fork at him. "Don't you think it's better for both genders to use both parts of their brains?"

Mac nodded. "Your argument has some interesting concepts, Ms. O'Gentry, but what does it have to do with my problem in Hangar 13?"

"It has to do with metaphysical law. The left brain's entire function is to keep our focus—our living, if you will—strictly channeled in this third-dimensional world. It has a filter that stops potential information from any other dimension from coming in and disrupting our reality."

Mac stared at her. "Okay, so far, so good. You're saying the left brain puts a certain kind of blinders on us, like you would on a horse pulling a carriage?"

"Exactly. The right brain has no such 'blinders' or filter in place, so it's open to receiving all the information that surrounds us, whether it can be seen with our physical eyes or not."

"What else is out there that the right lobe perceives?" Mac asked.

"Great question. Science acknowledges that we have at least three dimensions." Ellie touched the table with her long fingers. "We can see three sides to this table, so three dimensions are involved."

"Science would agree with you."

She smiled a little. "The right lobe can see into the fourth dimension, Mac, the one scientists don't want to confirm exists." She touched the middle of her forehead. "Remember earlier I told you that the right lobe's 'eye' was located here, the brow chakra?"

"Yes?"

"Well, if a person wants to, he can see *through* this table, which means he is viewing it through the fourth dimension. But he is 'seeing' with this invisible eye here in the center of his forehead. Anyone, with some work, can literally 'switch' to his right brain, close his eyes and do this."

Mac sat back, digesting the wild allegation. She obviously believed that what she was saying was the absolute truth. "I'm having a tough time buying this."

"Of course you are. Everything in your life has been predicated on left-brain ways. If you can't see it, weigh it or measure it, it doesn't exist. Yet—" Ellie smiled "—how do you explain dreams that come true, or a mother knowing her child is in danger or has been hurt before the phone call comes to validate it?"

"Okay...is that right-brain territory? Dreams? Telepathy?"

"Yes." She was pleased with his ability to catch on quickly. "People utilize their right lobe every day— they just don't realize it. As a shamaness, I have a special talent for using my right lobe. That's how I'm able to help people. And now," Ellie concluded, "back to the drawing board regarding your problem at Hangar 13." She found herself wanting to ask Mac a lot more personal questions, because despite his military background, and his very one-sided view of the world, he was trying to comprehend her world, too. She found that praiseworthy.

"The fourth dimension is already acknowledged by the scientific community," she went on. "Quantum physics is about that dimension. Our right brain has the capacity, the genetic setup, to see into that dimension, just as our physical eyes comprehend the first three dimensions. People like myself who have a strong genetic predisposition to right-brain activity, and who do a lot of personal work developing that lobe, can see into the dimension at will."

"How is it done?" Mac asked. His curiosity was piqued; he always liked exploring new territory, no matter where it was located.

"The right brain's ability to perceive the fourth dimension can be triggered in so many ways. For some, it's achieved through meditation. For others, through hallucinogenic drugs."

"And you?"

"A drum."

Mac gave her a blank look and saw her smile slightly.

"Native Americans, at least in North America, use the drum, a rattle, or a song or series of songs to create the proper vibrational environment that allows us to slip into the fourth dimension."

"So," he said, not at all sure he was putting the theory together properly, "you're saying this sound creates a doorway, a passage into the right lobe, where this opening is located?"

With a sigh, Ellie got up. "I wish everyone was as perceptive as you."

Mac sat back, content as never before. The sound of water running and dishes being piled in the sink lulled him pleasantly. "You are able to go into this fourth dimension with the sound frequency created by a drum?"

"Yes." Ellie pulled down a dish towel and placed it on the counter next to the sinks. "Come on, you can help dry, Major."

He grinned and stood up. "Considering the great meal, it's the least I can do."

Ellie met his very male smile. She noted how relaxed Mac had already become. He was like so many people when first confronted with metaphysics: threatened and ignorant. Once she was able to explain the process in nonthreatening terms, most people lost their wariness. She didn't expect Mac to believe her, but in order for her to answer the question he'd come to her to solve, he had to understand the basic mechanics of what she did.

As Mac stood beside her drying the dishes, he said, "So tell me—how does this all fit with the potential problem out in Hangar 13?"

CHAPTER THREE

Ellie scrubbed the skillet as she spoke. "Shamans—and shamanesses—have a very unique skill," she told Mac as he waited patiently at the sink, dish towel in hand. "We operate in the fourth dimension." She glanced up at him to register his reaction. "What we do is talk lost pieces of a person's soul into coming back to that person. That's what we call a healing."

"Pieces of your soul?" Mac gave her a very skeptical look.

"Don't judge what I'm saying yet," Ellie warned. She rinsed the skillet in hot water and handed it to him to dry. "Our belief embraces the possibility that people, as they go through life, lose pieces of themselves to another person or situation. If you're having trouble with the words *soul* or *spirit,* then consider it a loss of energy. People, when traumatized by a situation such as a divorce, the death of a loved one, the loss of a job or some other kind of tragedy, will very often lose a piece of themselves or their energy. Because of the shock, the 'piece' becomes stuck or lodged in that time period of their life."

Mac slowly dried the skillet, scowling. "Shock or trauma creates this condition?"

"Yes." Ellie took the bean pot and washed it. "And it's shock or trauma as perceived by the person, not by the world at large. For instance, a child of six falls off her bike and breaks her arm. Now, for an adult, this might not be such a shocking thing. But to the child, it's a horrible trauma. That little girl will, in all probability, lose a piece of herself.''

Mac shook his head. "What does this losing of pieces do, then?"

She smiled a little and handed him the rinsed pot. "With enough pieces of energy or spirit lost, people fall out of balance with themselves. It's a highly unconscious thing, but people who have suffered major soul loss begin to automatically rebalance in not-so-positive ways. A woman who gets divorced and loses a large piece of herself to her ex-husband may begin to binge on food, or drink, or be stuck emotionally in the past, never able to let go of that time in her life."

Mac put the pot aside and leaned thoughtfully against the counter. "Divorce is something I can understand," he said.

"Most of us do, unfortunately," Ellie said. She pulled the plug to drain the soapy water and rinsed her hands under the tap. Leaning over, she pulled a dry towel from a peg on the side of the cupboard and dried her hands. "There're a lot of what I call 'red flags' that tell me whether or not a person has lost a piece of himself—or herself—in a divorce."

"Such as?"

She smiled. "I can see I have your attention a hundred percent."

"I'm interested," Mac said, "but that doesn't mean I believe in this theory of yours."

With a shrug, Ellie motioned for him to sit down. She began to put the pots and pans away. "That's fine. I don't force anyone to believe as I do. But to me, a sign of soul loss is a person who cannot forget the divorce—the hurt, the anger or whatever negative feelings were created as a consequence."

Mac pulled out his chair and sat back down at the table. He could see dusk begin to settle outside the kitchen window, a few high clouds turned red-orange by the coming sunset. "I'd think it would be natural to have all those feelings after a divorce." He certainly did.

"Yes, but two or three years afterward? No, that's not healthy, Mac."

He scowled.

"Have you been able to adjust to it? Have you gotten on with your life? Or are you carrying the divorce around with you like a good friend?"

"Ouch." Mac rubbed his jaw. "My life hasn't been very good since Johanna divorced me," he admitted slowly.

"And you still think about it and her almost every day?"

He eyed her warily.

"I'm not being psychic, Mac. What I can tell you from my experience is that you two have taken pieces of each other. You're still living in the past with your ex-wife. You're probably wishing you had back the 'good old days' before the divorce happened."

He shrugged. "You're right...."

"That's a sign of soul loss." Ellie rested her hands on the table. "In a divorce where no pieces were taken by the partners involved, both are able to get on with their lives. They aren't constantly thinking about the partner, about their part in causing the divorce. They are able to live in the present and look to the future."

"Johanna divorced me," Mac admitted in a quiet voice. "I didn't want to, but..."

Gently, Ellie reached out and touched his arm. "Then, to correct this imbalance, I would tell you to have a shaman take a journey and check out the situation. Your ex-wife probably has a piece of you, and you have a piece of her. That's why the past is still living in the present with you."

Mac felt the brief touch of her fingers on his arm. His skin tingled pleasantly. He was sorry it was such brief contact. Ellie's eyes held such compassion for him and he sensed her sincerity. "You'd use your drum and do what?"

Rising, Ellie gestured for him to follow her. "Come on, I'll show you my healing room."

Highly curious, Mac followed her through her home. Down a hall, she opened the first door on the right. Mac stopped short, amazed. On the floor was a dark brown buffalo robe. A small table held a number of Native American items, including sage, a long brown-and-white feather and a pottery bowl that held ashes. More than anything, Mac was aware of the feeling in the room. At first, he pooh-poohed it, but as he moved toward the center of the room, an incredible sense of tranquility blanketed him.

Ellie quietly shut the door and moved to his side. She saw disbelief warring with what his senses were picking up about the room's energy. She leaned down

and retrieved a drum covered with elk hide. A butter-
fly was painted on it. "This is the drum I use when I
want to put myself into the right-brain state." She took
the drumstick and began to softly hit the instrument.

Mac felt the deep, low-throated sound coming from
the circular drum that Ellie held. At first, he consciously stopped himself from feeling anything, but as
the steady, monotonous beat filled the room, he
sensed something. And he saw a change in Ellie's eyes;
they became less sharp, seemed to lose their focus.

With a small laugh, Ellie stopped beating the drum
and set it back down against the wall. "If I keep playing it, I'll go into an altered state, and I don't want to."

Shoving his hands in his pocket, he turned and
looked around the rest of the room. There was a picture on the wall, and he went over to it. "Who are
these people?"

Ellie touched the dark frame of the picture. "The
woman in the middle is my mother, the other woman
is my sister Diana, and that's my father."

The woman in the middle had fierce black eyes; she
wore her gray hair in braids, but otherwise bore an
uncanny resemblance to Ellie. Mac studied her face for
a long time. Ellie's sister looked more like her father,
with lighter skin, dark brown hair and brown eyes.
The women were wearing some kind of ceremonial
clothes; the father was in a suit, looking proud. All of
them were smiling.

"This photo was taken on the day I got married,"
Ellie said reminiscently. "I had convinced my husband to let us get married on the reservation, with my
mother performing the ceremony." She sighed. "Ac-

tually, it was a compromise. Brian let my mother marry us, but then he demanded that a 'real' minister marry us off the reservation.''

Mac felt Ellie's sadness. ''He didn't believe in your mother's authority on the reservation?'' Mac gazed down at her and saw the pain in her eyes.

''No. Actually,'' Ellie admitted, ''that's why we eventually divorced. Brian couldn't accept my culture, what I do, the fact that I'm a shamaness and my life is devoted to the healing arts.''

''So the women of your family are doctors on the reservation?''

Her mouth twitched. ''We are called medicine people or healers. I let the medical doctors call themselves doctors. And there's a big difference between a healer and a doctor.''

''Such as?'' Mac took his hands out of his pockets.

''A healer, where I come from, is interested in the whole person, Mac. Modern doctors treat only a single piece or part, and address only the disease—not the issues that go into that state of imbalance. Healers take into account all the things about a person's life that may make them ill. There's a lot of common sense and practicality that comes into play, too.''

Ellie pointed to the buffalo rug. ''Let's take off our shoes and sit on down, shall we?''

Mac respected her request and placed his tennis shoes against the wall. He sat down cross-legged opposite Ellie. The robe was thick and silky feeling.

Ellie rested her arms on her crossed legs. ''I get people from all walks of life who have heard about me word-of-mouth. I journey for my clients in one of two ways, Mac. If they come and see me in person, we both lie down here on the robe together, side by side. I place my left hand over my client's right. I have a cassette of my drum being beaten, so I turn that on.'' She pointed to a small cassette player in the corner of the room. "I close my eyes and allow the drumbeat to make it easy for me to switch to the right brain, and then I move into the fourth dimension.''

"Can you feel it happen?''

"Sure. I'm consciously triggering the switch. It's important to know that a shaman is trained to turn it on and off at will, Mac. If we don't, then we're in big trouble. Let me give you an example. One of my clients—to protect the confidentiality of the healing, I'll call her Susan—was very sick. She had a major trauma in her past. So we lay down here together with the drum beating in the background. I asked my chief guide, who is a great blue heron, if I had permission to journey for Susan, and I was told yes. I flew on the back of my heron and we went down into what is known as the dark world, which is contained within Mother Earth. I was brought to a house and taken into a room. I saw Susan as a little five-year-old and I saw this man grab her.'' Ellie grimaced. "I won't share all the terrible details, but what I did see was Susan being sexually molested.''

Mac felt Ellie's emotional reaction to the scene. "You actually saw it?''

"Yes. You see, everything we've experienced in life is recorded, like film in the fourth dimension. My guide took me back to the time when Susan was emotionally traumatized, where she lost a huge piece of herself after being abused that way."

"What did you do?"

"I stopped the man from molesting her, separated them and asked Susan's little girl if she wanted to come home with me, back to the present Susan. She said yes, so I picked her up and we both rode back on my spirit guide."

Mac shook his head. "This sounds really weird, you know that?"

"Yes, I do. But before you judge me or the journey, wait until I tell you the outcome."

"Okay..."

"I brought back Susan's five-year-old, which really was a traumatic symbol of what had happened to her." Ellie patted the robe as she got to her knees. "Here, lie down here for a moment and I'll show you what I did, what I do to all my clients who want soul recovery."

Mac laid down on his back, his arms at his side. Ellie knelt by his left arm; she cupped her hands over his chest and lightly touched the region over his heart.

"A shaman will 'blow' the piece back into the person's heart and then sit the client up and blow the piece back into the top of his head." She leaned over Mac and pretended to blow into the circle of her cupped hands, which lay across his heart. Then she placed her hand beneath his neck and helped him sit up. Getting to her feet, she moved to his shoulder and cupped her hands once again, this time on the top of his head. Again she pretended to blow a piece into him. That done, she went to the table, where she picked up a rattle.

"Then I shake this rattle and move it around you four times." Ellie shook the rattle gently around Mac, noting his doubting expression. "You see, everything is living. This rattle is made out of a gourd, so it's alive. There are small pebbles gathered from an ant-hill in the rattle, and they're alive. As I bring this rattle around in a circle and shake it, I'm asking the spirits of the gourd and the stones to encircle you with protective gold light. We always do this after a recovery, because it ensures protection for the client for forty-eight hours afterward."

Ellie finished and sat down opposite Mac. She held the rattle gently in her hands. "Blowing a piece of someone's spirit back into them is like major surgery," she said. "The gold light put into place around you is like a dressing or bandage over the parts of you that experienced it, namely your heart and head."

Mac nodded. "This is pretty strange, Ellie."

Sadly, she nodded. "I know it is. The world I live in probably seems like another planet compared to yours."

"Yes," he admitted with a chuckle, "it does." And then his smile disappeared, because he saw the sadness in Ellie's eyes. "Your ex-husband didn't buy this," he said, gesturing around the room.

"No, and he knew what I did long before we married." She handled the rattle as if it were a child, slowly turning it between her hands. "I was young then. And idealistic. I thought love could conquer all." Glancing up at Mac, she saw the compassionate expression on his face. "I was wrong. My mother tried to warn me . . . but I wouldn't listen. I thought I knew better.''

"Head over heels in love?''

"Yes.'' Ellie fought the sudden tears and blinked them away.

Mac didn't miss the luminous look in her eyes. "If he didn't accept your beliefs, why did he marry you?''

"That,'' Ellie sighed, "is a long story.''

And one she obviously didn't wish to share with him. Mac could understand that. After all, he was a stranger who had walked into her life only a couple of hours ago. The funny thing about it was, Ellie didn't seem to be a stranger to him. He liked her. A lot. Silly beliefs or not, she was obviously a well-grounded, practical woman. Mac cast about for a safe topic.

"My marriage wasn't much better. Johanna met me here at Luke when I'd graduated from flight training. I think she was in love with the fighter-pilot image, not the man.''

Ellie nodded. Mac was an attractive man, not pretty-boy handsome, but he had a strong face, projected immense confidence, and she could see how a woman could be swayed by such a combination. "How long were you married?''

"Six years.''

"Me, too.''

Mac wanted to ask if there was anyone in her life presently. But he knew that was none of his business. Forcing a smile, he said, "So tell me, what happens after one of these healings?''

Relieved to be off a highly sensitive topic, Ellie said, "When I come back from a journey, I write down what I found. I turn off the drumming tape and we sit here talking. I told Susan what I saw, for example. She didn't relate to it nor did she remember being sexually molested.''

"Did Susan believe what you saw?''

Ellie shrugged. "It's not the shaman's responsibility to prove anything, Mac. I told her that now this piece of her had been returned, she would begin to integrate it back into her consciousness, and memories or dreams might occur. In the meantime, I suggested that she find a woman therapist to help her uncover her past.''

Mac just sat there, shaking his head. "I'm sorry. It's just such a farfetched concept.''

"It's strange, I know that.''

Mac shrugged. "I feel like I'm in an alien world.''

"That's okay. So, let's get back to your problem in Hangar 13.''

"Do you think it may be a lost piece of someone?'' Mac ventured, trying to see through her framework of reality.

"I don't know. It's possible, Mac. But it could be what we call a discarnate soul, the spirit of someone who has died but is refusing to leave to go to 'heaven,' and is staying around for a particular reason.''

"How can you tell?''

"I can't. Maybe if I go over to the hangar, I might be able to pick up on the energy. Maybe not. I can't 'see' particularly well when I'm not in that altered state.'' She touched her hair. "When I'm not journeying, I'm pretty much left brain, like you. So I'm 'blind' to the more-subtle vibrations of the fourth dimension that surround us."

"I've heard some people can see spirits or ghosts, though."

"Some can. I don't have that skill."

"But if you were in that altered state, you *could* 'see'?"

"That's right."

Mac nodded. "So you need to go to the hangar?"

"Yes, and we'll take the drum along."

He grimaced. "If my people heard a drum being beaten, they'd think I was crazy."

Ellie said nothing and watched the play of emotions on Mac's face. His large eyes reminded her of an eagle's piercing look. "I imagine you took a real chance just coming over to talk to me about it," she guessed wryly. "The metaphysical and military worlds don't usually have any common ground to walk upon."

"You've got that right," Mac muttered, bowing his head, his mind racing with possibilities.

"Is the hangar always in use?"

"Usually."

"We could go over when no one is there. That would save you the embarrassment of being 'found out.'"

Mac saw that her eyes were dancing with amusement. "I'm going up for early lieutenant colonel and the last thing I want is someone besides my master sergeant knowing that I've come to consult a psychic."

"A shamaness."

"Yes, whatever. If my superiors got wind of this, they'd send me to the nearest military hospital to check out my mental stability. But I've got to put an end to those wrenches flying around. I've got an IG—an inspector general's inspection—coming up in two months and I can't afford any problems. The hangar is empty right now. Could you come over with me and check it out?"

"You mean, feel my way through the hangar?"

"Yes. Maybe you'll get an impression or something."

Ellie hesitated and then nodded. "I'll try, but no promises. I'm blind as a bat when I'm not in an altered state to receive impressions."

"I'll take that risk." Rising from the robe, Mac held out his hand to Ellie. Her fingers wrapped firmly around his and he gently pulled her to her feet. The simple touch of her hand sent warmth racing up his arm. He tried to ignore the sensation. Releasing her hand, he said, "Thanks for taking the time with me. I appreciate it."

Ellie's hand tingled where Mac had held it. "You're welcome."

"What is your charge for doing a journey?"

"Whenever I do a journey for someone, I leave it up to them to give me what they can afford. It's on a donation basis only, Mac."

"But—"

"Healers operate from a very different perspective," Ellie interrupted, walking out of the room with him. "Unlike medical doctors, who expect financial compensation for their services, we often get other things in return."

"What do you mean?" Mac asked as he followed Ellie back into the living room.

"Well, a lot of my clients are either elderly or are single working mothers with children. Both are on very tight, fixed incomes." Ellie gestured for him to follow her into the kitchen. She opened the door to her pantry. "You see that row of canned fruit?"

Mac peered into the gloomy depths of the large, deep pantry and saw at least two dozen quart jars filled with various kinds of fruit. "Yes."

"One of my clients couldn't afford to pay me any money, so she gave me what she could."

Impressed, Mac eased out of the pantry. "I'll bet the electric company doesn't want to be paid in jars of fruit."

She laughed. "No, but you're missing my point. Not everyone who wants healing can afford the money, so I was taught to accept whatever gift the person had to give. On the reservation, it's common to bring groceries, blankets or other goods to the medicine woman. My mother often gave the groceries, the blankets and other items to the poor of our reservation because my father made a decent living as a plumber in the area."

"You were taught to be generous."

"Exactly. Being a healer means you live in the community and are a part of its fabric. I have another client who is very poor, but she came over and helped me plant my garden one evening. It was her way of paying me back for my services."

"I wish the rest of the world could operate on that kind of generosity."

"Like you said," Ellie murmured as she walked Mac to the front door, "the electric company doesn't want jars of fruit for payment. They want cold, hard cash."

Mac turned as he stepped out onto the front porch. "I like the world you live in."

"At least, that part of it."

Mac nodded and smiled slightly. "There's a lot to like about you, about your style of living," he told her seriously. "I may not believe in what you do, but I can respect you for it."

"That's all I ask."

"Then," Mac said, opening his hand toward her, "I'd like to 'pay' you for your services by taking you out to dinner sometime afterward. What do you say?"

CHAPTER FOUR

Ellie stared at Mac, her mouth dropping open. In the span of seconds, she ruthlessly scanned his eyes; they looked warm and sincere. His mouth was drawn into a slight, hopeful smile that she would say yes. Stunned by the offer, she scrambled for an answer.

"Major, I don't really think that's appropriate under the circumstances."

With a shrug, Mac said, "I think it is." For some reason, he was drawn to Ellie. He had surprised himself when the offer spilled from his lips, but after he'd asked her, he was glad. He could see the wariness in her eyes. Could he blame her for that kind of reaction, based on her past experiences with a man who didn't share her beliefs?

Compressing her lips, Ellie said, "I don't think so."

"Why?"

"Because we're from two very different worlds. I think you see that." She had made the biggest mistake of her life by marrying a white man who walked in a very different world than the one she had been raised in on the reservation. Ellie wasn't about to make the same mistake twice.

"I was raised to respect other people's ways of life."

Ellie shook her head. "I'll do what I can for you, for the problem you have in Hangar 13, but I think we should keep our relationship strictly professional." A part of her didn't want to and laughed at her words. But the past was still too poignant, too painful, for her to risk any other kind of friendship with him.

Mac waited on the front porch, while Ellie went to get her purse. Ruby-colored climbing roses encircled the two dark green trellises that leaned against either side of the porch. Their fragrance was subtle and sweet. The sun had set, and the sky looked as if it was on fire, a combination of red and red-orange, thinning out to a light peach color. For some unknown reason, he was happy. It was a mood he'd felt very little of lately—unless he was flying.

As Ellie quietly reappeared with her shoulder purse and a green shawl across her arm, Mac smiled at her. She was right—they were exact opposites. Ellie was grounded, rooted in the earth. He was an unfettered eagle who loved the air far more than the ground. And yet he couldn't help feeling some connection with her. He held his hand out.

"Want to ride over with me?"

Ellie looked at his hand. It was long and almost artistic looking. She had to remind herself that Mac Stanford was a throwback to another era. "Sure," she said, and allowed him to cup her elbow and guide her down the walk. Her skin tingled wildly where Mac gently held her arm.

"You remind me of a bygone time," Ellie told him, glancing up at his tall, proud form.

"Oh?"

"Military officers carry the weight of tradition on their shoulders. You're a true gentleman." Ellie felt him guide her toward a bright red sports car, a Corvette. She smiled to herself and thought the machine matched Mac's world. He flew hot jets. Why not drive a hot car?

Mac smiled absently and unlocked the passenger-side door for her. "You mean, the fact I'd open a door for you? Escort you?" He gestured for her to seat herself. Amusement danced in Ellie's eyes again, and he liked discovering how she thought or felt about things.

Ellie moved into the expensive, black leather seat. "I'm not saying you're the typical Neanderthal male trapped back in the cave."

With a chuckle, Mac shut the door. "That's reassuring." He moved around the rear of his sports car, opened the driver's door and climbed in. Putting on his seat belt, he glanced over at Ellie. Her lips were still pulled in a soft smile. "I was just curious how you saw me and my world," he said, easing the car away from the curb.

Ellie leaned back and enjoyed the ride in the sports car. It seemed appropriate that Mac was driving it; the instrument panel had a wraparound design, reminding her of the cockpit of an aircraft. "I think if this thing had wings, you'd fly it, too."

With a laugh, Mac nodded. "There are no secrets about me, are there?"

"Once an eagle, always an eagle," Ellie said. "You're always happier in the air."

"No argument there," Mac said. He turned off the boulevard and headed toward the interstate that would take them to Luke Air Force Base. The streetlights broke up the darkening sky, the coverlet of the night now stretching from horizon to horizon.

"What led you into the life of a military pilot?" Ellie asked. She wanted to know more about Mac. The fact he'd already asked her out on a date had startled her out of her normal response to men. Did he live fast? Had he asked her out from mere curiosity about her, or from genuine liking? Those were questions Ellie dared not ask.

Mac kept most of his attention on the nighttime traffic, which was diminishing now. "Since my father was an electrical engineer, I grew up helping him fix things around the house. He had always wanted to be a pilot, but had bad eyes and flat feet."

"So the military wasn't an option for him?"

"Right. He couldn't meet the physical qualifications."

"But he passed on his love of flying to you?"

"Yes. He took me to the airport at least once a year and I saw the Air Force Thunderbirds fly. I knew when I was ten what I wanted to be."

"A bird," Ellie said.

Mac glanced at her and smiled. "Exactly."

"Birds can fly above a situation and not get involved."

"That's an interesting observation," he murmured.

"We all have our escape routes when things get bad or too painful for us to cope with." Ellie opened her hands. "Look at me. When I'm unhappy or in pain, I work in my garden for a couple of hours and I come away feeling much better."

"Oh," Mac said. "And do you view this escapism as a cop-out?"

"Not necessarily. I see going to the garden as something positive, something life affirming. I'll bet when things get bad around your office, you take off and go fly. When you come back, you feel better. Right?"

He chuckled. "You've got me all figured out, haven't you? You're right, of course—flying is more than just a simple pleasure for me. It's also an escape valve." His brows dipped. "Right now, with all my work pressures and this trouble at Hangar 13, I've been wanting to grab my g-chaps and helmet and fly all the time."

"Sure, you'd like to leave it behind."

"Flying helps me think more clearly," Mac said. He met and held her luminous eyes. "Does gardening do the same thing for you?"

"You bet it does."

"Maybe we're not so different after all."

Ellie chuckled. "I'm a ground person and you're an air person—we're not exactly similar."

"But we derive the same things out of our experience."

With a nod, Ellie conceded his point.

"Just because people are opposites doesn't necessarily mean they can't get along," Mac added.

"Is that argument for my benefit or yours?"

He laughed. It was a deep, rolling laugh, and he hadn't laughed like that for a long, long time. "You're a pleasant surprise to my world, Ms. O'Gentry."

"Thank you, Major." Her smile lit up her face.

"Can you say the same about me, I wonder?"

"You're a surprise," Ellie said. "Can we leave it at that?"

"For now." He chastised himself for moving too quickly with Ellie. She was cautious, and he couldn't blame her. What had gotten into him, anyway? It had been a long time since he'd entertained the thought of having a woman in his life. Since the divorce, Mac had thrown himself into his work—usually twelve-hour days—to forget the pain from the past.

"So you grew up in Portland. You were a city kid. When did you learn to fly?"

"My father paid for my flying lessons and I had a student pilot's license when I was seventeen."

Ellie was impressed. "And what made you choose the air force?"

"I enrolled in the Air Force Academy because it was my father's favorite military service."

"So your father was pretty much living out his unfulfilled dream through you."

"That's right."

"And you didn't mind?" Ellie wondered what might have happened to Mac if he hadn't been so strongly influenced by his father.

"No. It was just sort of a natural progression, I suppose."

"Is there anything else you wanted to do besides fly?"

Mac slowed down and took the off ramp leading to the air base. The sky was completely black now. Luke sat west of Phoenix, and he could see the thousands of stars quilted into the fabric of the sky. "When I get a chance, I like to hike in the desert."

"Oh?"

"I like to hunt for rocks."

"Really?" So there was a streak of earth in him!

"I'm an amateur rock hound of sorts," Mac said hesitantly as they approached the main entrance of Luke Air Force Base.

"An eagle who likes rocks. Isn't that a bit of a dichotomy?"

Mac braked the sports car at the main gate. "I don't know. Is it?"

Smiling, Ellie said nothing. She saw the sentry, dressed in a light blue, short-sleeved shirt, and dark blue slacks, snap to rigid attention and salute Mac as he slowly drove past onto the base. The base seemed quiet and Ellie couldn't see much in the darkness.

"What do you know about Luke?" Mac asked as he navigated through the streets toward the hangars silhouetted in the distance.

"Not much. You don't learn a lot about the military when you're raised on a reservation."

"I see." Mac swung the car down another street and drove toward the last hangar silhouetted in the darkness.

"I'm opposed to war," Ellie told him. "Men have waged too many wars over the centuries and no good ever comes from it. Everybody suffers."

"No argument from me." Mac eased into a parking space next to the huge, dark hangar. "I see myself as a deterrent to war."

"Really?" Ellie eyed him questioningly. "Were you in Desert Storm?"

"Yes." Mac turned off the engine. Silence settled as he turned and gazed at her shadowed face. "Being in the military doesn't give us the right to decide who's right or wrong. We're in place to protect this country and its people."

With a sigh, Ellie said, "I'm not a warrior like you, Mac. I have real reservations about the military in general."

He opened the door; he didn't want to open that can of worms. "This is Hangar 13. Come on, I'll take you inside and you can check out where I work."

With a nod, Ellie got out before Mac could come around and open the door for her. Not to be deterred, Mac cupped her elbow and led her along the sidewalk that curved around to the front of the hangar. Ellie noticed he deliberately shortened his long, lanky stride to match hers.

"Tonight there's no one working in the hangar," he said, gesturing toward it.

The place looked like an oversize Quonset hut to Ellie. Lights illuminated the top of it.

"We repair the jets from our squadrons in these hangars," he explained as he opened the door for her.

Ellie nodded. Once inside the huge, shadowy structure, she said, "Let me just stand here for a moment and accustom myself to the vibrations." The bay area was nearly dark. Two huge F-15 fighters sat quietly, ready to be worked on come morning. No unusual sounds disturbed the silence.

Mac nodded and dropped his hand from her elbow. "I can turn on more lights if you want."

"No...this is fine." Ellie took a deep breath to center herself. With Mac's presence, it was tougher than usual for her to focus inwardly. She liked him, despite his career calling. And, to be honest, she found him more than a little attractive. Still, a voice in the back of her head told her, there was no room in her personal life for a military officer. They could never hope to find a common meeting ground.

Mac stepped aside and watched Ellie as she closed her eyes. Her lashes lay like thick ebony fans against her high, golden cheekbones. She had placed her shawl around her shoulders and stood with her hands clasped against her breast. She bowed her head slightly, eyes still shut. He wondered what she was doing.

Taking deep breaths through her nose and releasing them through her mouth, Ellie was able to center herself, to switch to her internal guidance, which connected her gut, her heart and her right brain. Everything had a feeling to it, a frequency, and as she opened herself up to all possibilities, she allowed the feelings of the hangar to permeate her consciousness. The silence was almost oppressive to her. Then, suddenly, she felt movement.

Opening her eyes, she turned quickly toward Mac. "Did you move?"

"No. Why?"

Ellie shrugged and tried to pierce the gloomy depths of the hangar. "I felt movement. I thought it was you."

He looked around, his brow wrinkling. "Where did the movement come from?"

Ellie pointed to the far corner of the hangar. "Over there."

Mac scowled. "That's where the tools are always thrown from."

With a sigh, she nodded. "Good, then my senses are working."

"What did you see?"

"Nothing. I *felt* movement. A fast, quick move, that's all."

Impressed and curious, Mac said nothing. Ellie was looking around the hangar, her mouth set, her eyes narrowed. She wrapped the shawl a little more tightly around her shoulders.

"I'm not a clairvoyant," she told him. "I don't 'see' things. I can only sense feeling or movement, that's all."

"But when you're in the journeying state, you can see?"

"I see in symbolic form, usually." Ellie shrugged. "I need to tell you more of how I perceive things in the fourth dimension, but there's no use doing that unless you want me for this job."

Mac nodded. Even though he'd just met her, he knew Ellie was the kind of woman he'd trust with his life in an emergency. She had an incredible sense of grounding and stability he'd rarely seen in anyone, man or woman. "Sure, I want you to help me with this problem if you can."

"Okay...." Ellie gestured toward the center of the bay. "Just let me walk around, Mac. I want to feel my way around this hangar. You can follow about six feet behind me. If you get too close, I'll start picking up on your aura vibration and that will confuse what else I'm feeling and sensing."

He nodded. "Go ahead. I'll hang back."

Instinctively, Ellie wanted to head straight for that one particular corner, but she stopped herself from doing that. "You see, every square inch of Mother Earth has vibration, feeling," she told him, pointing toward the concrete floor of the hangar. "Most people don't feel it—a lot of animals do, but we don't."

"Why?"

"We're too locked into the third dimension," Ellie said as she slowly started to walk around the perimeter of the hangar.

Mac hung back as he'd promised. The silence was overwhelming to him. He didn't like it. Ellie would walk about ten feet, halt, close her eyes and stand there. She would take several deep breaths and wait. For what, he didn't know. Perhaps that feeling or energy she had talked about. Some kind of subtle impression? Whatever it was, he tried to feel, too, but came up with nothing.

As Ellie moved toward the last corner, she felt a chill, the briefest shift of energy. Then, halfway down the side of the hangar, she felt a powerful movement. Her eyes flew open and she stared into the gloom.

"What is it?"

Mac's voice held a tinge of urgency, and she felt his instant concern. Turning, she looked up at his shadowed features. "Did you feel that?"

He shook his head. "No, nothing...."

Slowly turning, Ellie said, "I felt movement again, only this time it was very obvious."

"What does that mean?"

"I don't know," she whispered, her hands tightening on the shawl. "I'll have to go into the corner and try to figure it out."

"Look," Mac said, "be careful."

She smiled over her shoulder. "I thought you didn't believe in paranormal activity, Major."

He frowned. Ellie was right. So what was he reacting to? He hadn't felt any movement, no sense of dread. With a shrug, he muttered, "It's just my protective nature coming out."

Her mouth curved slightly. "That's okay." And it was. Ellie knew that many people who hadn't developed the sensing abilities of their right lobe were still sensitive. If Mac flew these huge, powerful planes, he had to have some kind of instinct working for him. Whether he called it a hunch or explained it away with some left-brain rationalization didn't matter to Ellie. What did matter was that Mac had, somehow, sensed the movement, too.

The energy she was tuning in to suddenly tightened. Ellie stopped again and closed her eyes. Again she felt movement, but this time it was different. She opened her eyes and slowly turned her head toward Mac.

"I think you'd better stay back."

"Why?"

"Because what I'm sensing isn't positive."

"What do you mean?" Mac had to stop himself from walking up to Ellie.

She pointed to the corner, about a hundred feet away from them. "The energy is different here."

"Explain."

"It's tighter." She opened her hands. "It's as if there's a sense of fear, of threat. That's the best I can do to explain the change, Mac."

"Why would it be different?"

"I haven't the slightest idea." At least, not yet. Ellie walked another twenty feet. This time she didn't need to close her eyes to feel the energy shift. A swirling, muddied sensation blanketed her briefly, then moved away, deeper into the corner. She held out her hand to Mac.

"Stay back. Don't follow me."

Frustrated, Mac halted, his hands jammed into the pockets of his pants. A part of him, the disbeliever, wondered if Ellie was making all of this up. If she was, she was a very good actress. Her voice had grown husky, with an edge of warning in it. Another part of him wondered, though, if something really was going on that he couldn't see or perceive. Facts warred with fiction in his head. Mac didn't want to believe that anything paranormal existed. Still, if it didn't, why would Ellie be going to all this trouble? It wasn't as if she made a fortune from her shamanistic work. Confused, he watched as she moved forward with new caution.

She halted fifty feet from the corner of the hangar. Her skin prickled in warning, and the hair on the back of her neck stood up as a chill blanketed her. With her eyes, she tried to pierce the gloom. She saw nothing. There was an urgency, a real threat surrounding her.

Closing her eyes, she tried to center herself. The energy was antagonistic. Threatening. Danger was near. What kind? What? She tried to remain quiet inwardly, for to lose her center, her balance, would put her in danger if there was something here whose intent was to hurt—or kill.

As she closed her eyes, Ellie switched to the "screen" in the center of her forehead. Unless she was in that altered state, she received no picture or symbols. All she could see was darkness. Her heart began to beat a little harder, and she fought to remain centered. Something was moving. Moving ... Turning silently to the right, Ellie followed the feeling of movement. Anger. White-hot anger deluged her. She felt her entire physical body shudder in the wake of it. Hatred. She drew in a deep, steadying breath of air.

"Ellie! Look out!" Mac's voice caromed throughout the hangar like thunder.

Startled, she jerked her eyes open.

Mac lunged for Ellie. He managed to strike her shoulder, and she let out a little cry as she lost her balance. As he jerked her into his arms, steadying her, something large sailed past them. It struck the concrete with a sharp, pinging sound.

"What?" Ellie whispered unsteadily. She regained her balance, wildly aware of Mac's strong arms around her.

He stared at the corner, shocked. "Did you see that?"

"What?" Ellie stood on her own and his hands dropped from her shoulders. She stared into the gloom.

"This." Mac went over and picked up a screwdriver. "Didn't you see it?"

"N-no." Ellie took the long, narrow screwdriver from him.

Scratching his head, Mac said in disbelief, "I saw it hanging in thin air. Somehow, I knew it was going to be thrown—at you." He stared at her startled expression. "This is crazy," he whispered angrily. "No screwdriver can hang in midair!"

Ellie said, "Let's move away from this corner. I'm still getting chills. It isn't safe, Mac. I don't care whether you believe me or not."

He wasn't sure what he believed at this point. Gripping Ellie's arm, he pulled her back toward the door. At least there was more light there, and he felt safer. The screwdriver was real. Who had thrown it? *What* had thrown it? There was no one else in the hangar right now, Mac was sure of it. He had no answers and he felt angry. Ellie could have been hurt! If he hadn't seen the tool dangling in midair above her, who knows what might have happened?

Shaken, Ellie halted at the door beneath the light. The screwdriver felt cold in her hands and she shivered.

"Stay here," Mac muttered.

"Wait!" She made a grab for his arm. "What are you going to do?"

"I'm going back over there," he said. "*Somebody* has to have thrown that screwdriver."

"No! Don't go over there, Mac! Believe me, there's a malevolent spirit there. He could attack you if you get too close. Please, don't go...."

Mac shook his head. "Stay here, Ellie. I'll be back in a minute."

Smothering her protest, she waited where she was. Mac moved with frightening swiftness back across the hangar. She lost sight of him as he moved around one of the jets and disappeared into the gloom. Her heart was beating raggedly in her breast. She was worried for Mac, but there was little she could do. He didn't believe what he'd seen, and now he was looking for a physical culprit to blame it on. Ellie knew he'd find no one.

Ten minutes later, Mac came back, his face set, his eyes narrowed. Ellie stood under the light at the entrance, the shawl tight around her tense shoulders. She looked pale, her huge eyes holding fear. As he approached her, he muttered, "I didn't find anyone."

"I know...."

He scowled and reached out for her, his hand resting on her shoulder. He could feel the tension in her. "How are you?"

She smiled a little. "Shaken up, but okay. What happened over there?"

"Nothing."

"Good."

He shook his head. "Come on, let me take you home."

"Thanks...." Once they left the hangar and were outside beneath the starlit sky, she felt better. Mac kept his hand on her elbow, and this time, she was glad for his closeness.

"I don't know what happened in there," he said tightly. "I saw it, but I don't believe what I saw."

Ellie nodded and allowed him to open the door of the Corvette for her. She waited until he got inside and they were driving away from the hangar before she spoke.

"If you hadn't yelled, I'd never have seen that screwdriver."

"Your eyes were closed. I knew you couldn't see it."

"Well," Ellie whispered, feeling very shaky in the aftermath, "I'm glad you saw it."

His mouth quirked. "Someone had to have thrown it at you. Damn."

"Mac, the person who threw it wasn't physical. You're going to have to accept that sooner or later." She saw the stubborn set of his jaw. "Whatever is in that hangar is angry, and is carrying a lot of hatred."

"How do you know?"

"I felt it."

The sentry at the gate again saluted smartly. Once outside the gate, Mac pressed on the gas and the Corvette speeded down the road. "Did you see anything?"

"No," Ellie said sadly. "I can see only when I'm in that altered state. What I sensed was like a storm, a big, powerful storm. The closer I got to the corner, the more the energy became agitated, threatening and powerful."

"This is crazy!"

Ellie said nothing. She could feel Mac wrestling with what had happened. "What do you want to do about it?" she asked him finally once they were on the freeway heading toward her home.

Snorting softly, Mac said, "Forget the whole thing."

"You can't do that."

He glared at her. "Why not?"

"Because your people are being injured by whatever is in that corner. And I've got news for you—whatever or whoever it is, is not going to stop hurling tools at your people, Mac. Sooner or later, it could do serious damage. Is that what you want? Do you want your people really hurt? Maybe killed?"

"This is just too much for me to believe, Ellie."

"I know it is," she whispered. Her smile was sad. "I was afraid your traditional world would crash into mine, into what I know about this kind of paranormal phenomenon."

"I respect what you believe," he told her firmly. "But it's a whole other thing for *me* to believe it."

"Mac, I think I know enough about you to say this—your concern for the people who work for you will override your disbelief of what you saw."

Rubbing his jaw, he glanced over at Ellie. She looked serene once again; the fear had left her eyes, and her mouth was soft and without tension. "All right," he rasped, "when we get back to your place, you lay it out for me—give it to me with both barrels. It really doesn't matter what I believe anymore. I've got to keep my people safe."

CHAPTER FIVE

Ellie went to the kitchen and turned on the water to wash her hands. She felt Mac's agitation as he hovered nearby.

"I don't know about you," Mac said, "but I could use a drink."

Ellie pointed to the refrigerator. "There's some white zinfandel in there. Pour us each a glass."

It was a good idea. As Mac pulled out the wine, he kept an eye on Ellie. She seemed far less upset about the evening then he did.

"You seem cool, calm and collected," he muttered, pouring the wine into two crystal goblets.

With the towel, she patted her palms dry. "Mac, this is a world I'm used to. You're not, so it shakes you up. Sit down."

He sat and she joined him.

She raised her glass. "Here's to your indoctrination into metaphysics."

With a snort, he gently touched her goblet with his. "I know what I saw. I just don't want to believe it."

"I know it's a shock to you," Ellie said wryly, sipping the cool, sweet wine.

With a shake of his head, Mac said, "It's not my world."

Setting the goblet aside, Ellie gave him a compassionate look. "Let me explain what I think happened. It's a professional guess, but I really won't know for sure until I go back in there and check it out in my altered state."

"Okay," Mac said. "What do you think is going down?" He worried about his crews, who would be coming in that morning at 0600. What if another screwdriver was thrown at them? His mind raced with more questions than he had answers for.

"I believe there is a discarnate spirit living in your hangar."

"That's a spirit that's died but hasn't gone to heaven?"

"Yes, so to speak. There is a place where most spirits go after they've left the physical body after death. Some spirits stay behind because they miss a loved one, or because they miss something as simple as a favorite food, smoking or drinking. I once was asked to investigate a spirit who had been seen in an orchard, and when I journeyed and talked to him, I found out it was the owner who had originally planted that orchard. He loved his fruit trees so much, and was so worried that the present owner of the place wouldn't take care of them, that he chose to stay and guard them himself." She saw the disbelief on Mac's face. "I know this all sounds crazy to you, but it's the truth."

"Go on," Mac said unhappily.

"I was able to talk to that spirit and convince him that the present owner of the house would take good care of his trees, that they'd be well cared for. Once the spirit was convinced, he left, went on into what we call the light world, or heaven."

"And you think that what is in the corner of Hangar 13 is one of these spirits?"

"I think so." Ellie shrugged. "But there's a danger to this, whatever it is."

"No kidding." Shaking his head, Mac put is glass aside. "I saw the screwdriver just hanging there in midair, Ellie. At first I didn't believe it, but then this feeling came over me, and I knew it was going to be thrown at you."

"So you reacted on a feeling," Ellie said, pleased. "You were making decisions based upon your intuition, not your logic." He didn't seem quite so happy about it. Reaching out, she briefly touched his hand. "Usually, your world and my world don't overlap, Mac. But you've got something out in your hangar that isn't physical. What it's *doing* is physical, though, and we have to do something about it. And fast."

Mac liked the firm, warm touch of Ellie's hand on his. "What's really got me going is the fact that there are never any tools left around the hangar. Each crew member has his own set and they're put away at the end of the day. You saw how clean and empty the hangar floor was. There weren't any tools lying around."

"If a spirit is powerful enough, Mac, it can literally create what it wants and manifest it into this third dimension. I'm sure it manifested that screwdriver."

Exasperated, he glanced at her. "What would you do about this?"

"Let's go back tomorrow night, providing no one is working in there. You can beat the drum for me, and I'll go into an altered state and find out more about what is in that corner."

Mac thought about what would happen if anyone on base found him beating a drum in the darkened hangar. It would be embarrassing, at the very least. But he couldn't ignore the sincerity in Ellie's eyes. With a sigh, he smiled slightly and said, "The last crew leaves at 2100—I mean, nine p.m. How about if I come over and pick you up to be there around midnight? Everyone should be gone by that time, and it will be quiet."

"Good, because if the drumming is interrupted, Mac, it puts me in danger."

"How?"

"The drum is like a road, a passage for me," Ellie said. "The beat, the vibration, provides a path to and from my altered state. Shamans can get into real big trouble if they get 'stuck' in what we term nonordinary reality."

"You mean, if I quit beating the drum, you could be stuck?"

"Yes."

"What would happen then?"

"I'd be in either an unconscious or a semiconscious state, and nothing on this earth could bring me out of it."

"Except the drumbeat?" Mac guessed.

"Yes." Ellie smiled. "You catch on fast. The other alternative would be to have another shaman journey on my behalf, to help me come out of that state and back into this reality."

"How long do I beat this drum of yours?"

"I'm fairly fast at journeying, so usually no more than fifteen minutes. Tomorrow, I'll show you how to beat the drum. It's not hard."

"Good," Mac said. He reached over and gently held her hands.

Mac's touch was galvanizing, and Ellie felt the strength and the warmth of his fingers. Her heart speeding up, she pulled her hand from his. There was such magnetism between them! But it was wrong, all wrong.... Her lifestyle was a threat to him.

"I guess I'd better get going," Mac said, slowly rising. "It's been a long day and a real interesting night."

Ellie nodded and stood. "It's probably going to get more interesting tomorrow night."

At the front door, Mac hesitated. The lamplight from the living room bathed Ellie's oval face and high cheekbones in a radiant glow. He found himself wanting to tunnel his fingers through her thick, black hair. But he knew he had no business doing that. Ellie's profession was a part of her, and Mac didn't know how to deal with that—at least not yet. He gave her a warm look. "I'll pick you up tomorrow night at eleven."

Ellie felt his inspection, felt the heat flowing through her as he appraised her with those hazel eyes so alive with intelligence. She wished she had met Mac under different circumstances. Sadness flowed through her. It was obvious he was wrestling with her life-style. Unless he was able to accept it—not necessarily embrace it, but at least respect it—Ellie knew it was pointless to hope for any kind of personal relationship with him.

After Mac said good-night and disappeared into the darkness, Ellie closed the door quietly. She liked his steadiness, his intelligence and obvious warmth. If only... Ellie shook away her thoughts and headed for the bathroom to run a tub of water.

But the sadness returned as she added lilac-scented bath salts to the warm water. She couldn't get Mac out of her mind, and she laughed softly. Look at them— she a shamaness, he a military officer. Could they be any more opposite? She knew that some men were drawn to her unusual life-style, but their interest had never extended to the person Ellie was inside. What made her think Mac would be any different?

Sitting on the edge of the pink tub, she moved her hand gently through the warm water to dissolve the bath crystals. What did Mac really think of her? Did he see only her profession? Was that the focus of his interest in her? Or did he see beyond what she did for a living, to the person she was? Ellie wasn't sure at all.

At the moment, though, they had more pressing issues to deal with. Whether or not Mac believed in spirits, there was one in Hangar 13, and it posed a real threat to the people who worked there. Ellie hoped that she could find more answers tomorrow night— before anyone else got hurt.

"Are you ready?" Mac's voice echoed eerily throughout the gloomy depths of Hangar 13. It was a little past midnight, and he had just brought out two chairs from his office for them to sit on. Ellie was dressed in a white cotton skirt and a soft pink shell, and had a beautifully crocheted dark pink shawl draped around her proud shoulders. Tonight she wore her hair loose and free, and Mac was having trouble keeping his attention—and his hands—off her and on the situation.

"Yes." Ellie took one of the chairs and sat down, facing the corner furthest from the one where she'd sensed the agitation, anger and hatred. This was the safest place for her to commence her journey. She planted her sandaled feet firmly on the concrete floor of the hangar. All was quiet—almost too quiet. Glancing up, she saw Mac standing nervously a few feet away. She beckoned for him to join her.

Mac took the other folding chair and sat down about two feet away from her, the drum in one hand, the drumstick in the other. "I feel kind of silly," he admitted.

Ellie smiled. "No one is going to come by and catch you playing a drum, Mac, so relax." She couldn't blame him for his nervousness. She was a bit tense herself. And with Mac sitting so close, she was finding it a little hard to concentrate. He was dressed in formfitting jeans that revealed his long legs and a red polo shirt that outlined his upper body to perfection. But Ellie had to focus on what was before them.

He tested the drum, creating a steady, sonorous beat that echoed and reechoed throughout the hangar. Looking up, he saw her nod.

"That's a good, steady beat. Just keep doing it until I tell you to stop."

"Okay." It was a round drum and fairly heavy, and the twelve elk-skin thongs converged in the center so that Mac could easily hold it in his hand. He watched with curiosity as Ellie folded her hands in her lap, took a deep breath and closed her eyes. What would she find? What would she see? Mac had no idea what to expect, but he was watchful of that corner where he'd seen the screwdriver suspended last night. The hangar was shadowy and gloomy, the lights overhead throwing dark, distorted shapes here and there. If he wasn't careful, he would start seeing things in those shapes....

Ellie began to breathe deeply and evenly. The drum's resonance was at once soothing and focusing. She could feel the vibration begin to permeate her. Mac's presence was disconcerting, and she had to hone in and concentrate even more to achieve the proper state.

Suddenly, Ellie could feel herself switching from the left hemisphere of her brain to the right. The viewing screen in front of her closed eyes instantly brightened, and a moment later, her spirit guide, an Indian woman known as Yona, which meant "bear" in Cherokee, appeared to her. She was dressed in a soft deerskin dress, her braids thick and black.

"It is good to see you again, my friend," Yona greeted.

Ellie saw herself approaching her guide, who was not only her mentor, but her friend as well. *"Osiyo,"* Ellie said, which meant hello in Eastern Cherokee. She embraced Yona and felt an instant warmth and unending love surround her. As she stepped back, El-

lie said, "I would like permission to journey on behalf of Major Mac Stanford."

Yona nodded gravely. "You have our permission,
Iya."

Ellie nodded. Her given Eastern Cherokee name was
Iya, which meant "pumpkin." To an ordinary person, it was a funny name that always drew a smile. But
it symbolized something much deeper. A pumpkin
held seeds of possibility, and her mother had always
told her she was a woman of many skills and talents.
A pumpkin was close to Mother Earth, one of her
vegetables, rounded and pregnant looking. Her
mother had always said, that Ellie was filled with
many brain children or ideas.

"Is there anything I need to know going into this
journey?" she asked Yona.

"It will be dangerous, but your spirit-guide animals will protect you. Go carefully, my sister."

Ellie thanked her. She found herself flanked with a
number of animals that existed in the spirit realm of
the fourth dimension. A shamaness had no defenses
of her own, so had to rely upon a vanguard of soldiers, who took the shape of animals, to be her pro-
tectors. Ellie saw her gray wolf and leaned over and
patted the animal, who wagged her tail in joyful ac-
knowledgment. A golden eagle sat nearby, her yellow
eyes fierce, and Ellie went over and patted her lovingly on the head.

Her third friend and protector was a mountain lion,
who rubbed and purred against her legs. Ellie thanked
Yona and asked her spirit guides to take her to the
corner of Hangar 13. Ellie would never undertake a

journey without direct permission; to do otherwise indicated disrespect for the situation.

It was easy to move in the fourth dimension. In the blink of an eye, she was standing in the corner of the hangar, far above the floor. Ellie looked around. She could see herself sitting in the chair, and she could see Mac beating the drum. Hearing the growl of her mountain lion, Ellie turned, startled. Her heart began beating harder. In the corner, she saw a dark, churning cloud, looking like an approaching thunderstorm. The roiling black-and-gray cloud wove in and out, like hundreds of snakes slithering quickly in and around one another. The sensation was one of pure danger. Instantly, the cougar placed herself between Ellie and the approaching menace.

"Stop," Ellie shouted, and threw up her hand. The cloud was at least ten feet high and twenty feet wide. She felt the anger and hatred and shock. The storm stopped. The cougar growled warningly.

"Whoever you are, come out of hiding. I'm Iya, and I've come to speak to you. I mean you no harm."

She stood there, feeling the wolf on her left and the eagle on her right. Out of the thick, moving clouds, she saw a dark shape emerge. It hung there, only partly visible.

"I come in peace," Ellie told the spirit, which took the vague shape of a human.

"Go away!"

The voice, deep and furious, buffeted Ellie. She took a step back, feeling scorched by the spirit. "I can't. I need to find out why you're here in this hangar. Why are you throwing tools at the people who work here? They are innocent. What can I do to help you and them?"

The dark shape moved out of the clouds, drifting to the left. Ellie tried to see its face, but there was none to see. She sensed it was male. "Will you speak with me?" she pleaded.

"No! Get out of here! This is *my* place! You have no business coming here! If you don't go, I'll kill you!"

"I've only come to help you if I can."

"Help me?" roared the spirit. "Find my killer!"

Stunned, Ellie stood there, feeling the spirit's utter fury. "You were murdered? By whom? Can you tell me what happened?"

"Bah!"

"First, you must promise me you will leave these people alone. Will you?" She felt his malevolent glare. "Well?" she goaded.

"Yes! I will not harm them while you hunt for my murderer."

The spirit slipped back into the roiling clouds.

Ellie stood there for a long time. The cougar remained crouched, her tail twitching, and she knew it was a sign that the spirit was capable of attacking her.

"Spirit, can you tell me your name?"

There was no response. Ellie turned to her spirit guides. "Will he come out and talk to me?"

The eagle shook her head. "He thinks you are coming to take his territory from him. He's dangerous. Let us go from here."

Ellie always listened to her spirit guides; they possessed wisdom she did not and were there to help her understand the sometimes-confusing energy found in the fourth dimension.

"Okay. Thanks, gang. I'll see you later." She patted each one of them and saw herself coming back to where she was sitting in the chair. Ellie saw herself slipping back into her physical body, and as she did, she felt heavier. Gradually, as she returned to the third dimension, the beating of the drum became louder. The feeling of heaviness remained, and she knew she was back to the here and now. Lifting her lashes, she raised her hand and signaled to Mac to stop drumming.

Mac stopped and set the drum aside. He studied Ellie's eyes. They were out of focus, but within a minute they became sharp and lively looking once again. He stopped himself from demanding to know what had gone on—if anything.

Ellie sat up in the chair, rubbed her hands along her thighs and took a long, deep breath of air. "The spirit promised to stop hurting people if we did one thing for him."

"What's that?"

"Do you know if someone was murdered here in Hangar 13?"

The question caught Mac completely off guard. "Murdered?"

"Yes." Ellie motioned toward the corner. "Mac, this spirit is male. He wouldn't let me see his face. All I saw was a dark shape of a man. He's very angry, and he's dangerous. When I asked what happened, he said, 'Find my murderer.'" She tilted her head and saw the shock in his expression. "How long has Hangar 13 been here?"

"It was built six months ago. It's the newest hangar on Luke." Mac shook his head. "Murder? I don't know what I expected, Ellie, but not that."

She stood up and stretched. "Sometimes when a person is killed suddenly and without warning, his spirit remains in the spot where his life was taken." She looked around the hangar. "Do you know of any murders that took place on base?"

"No..."

"Are you sure? How about an accidental death?" Ellie walked over and picked up the drum. "It doesn't necessarily have to be murder."

Mac got up and folded both chairs. He carried them back to the office where he'd gotten them. Ellie followed along silently. Inside the office, he placed the chairs in the corner and turned to her. His expression was thoughtful.

"I guess I can give the provost marshal a call tomorrow and check it out."

"Okay." Ellie could see him struggling with the information. "I'm sorry I couldn't get more from the spirit, Mac."

He shrugged and cupped her elbow. Guiding her out of the office, he asked, "How are you feeling?"

"A little lightheaded, but that's normal after coming back," Ellie assured him.

"Does it last long?"

"Maybe fifteen or twenty minutes. I don't drive during that time, believe me."

"Sort of like taking eight or nine g's," he murmured, opening the outer door of the hangar for her. "Those are units of gravity a pilot is often exposed to taking off in a high-speed aircraft."

"Oh?" Ellie enjoyed walking beside him. The peaceful night seemed such a contrast to the turmoil she had just witnessed. The sky overhead was dark and sparkling with stars. She heard a couple of jets taking off in the distance, the silence broken by their ominous, powerful rumble.

"I ought to take you up in my bird someday soon," he said. "You could get a taste of my world." Grinning, he added, "I won't make you take eight or nine g's, though."

"I've never flown except in a commercial jet," Ellie admitted. She saw the light in Mac's eyes, a light of joy.

He led her to the car and opened the door for her. "Would you?"

Ellie halted at the door and looked up into his darkly shadowed features. "What?"

"Fly with me?"

"Well . . ."

"We're always flying media types for public relations purposes. Just last week we had the Thunderbird flying team in here. How about it? I'd like to show you a little of what I do." Never had Mac wanted a woman to say yes more than now. He saw the wariness come back into Ellie's eyes. Was she comparing him to her ex-husband? His hand tightened on the door, and he unconsciously held his breath.

"I don't know. . . ."

"Is this reverse prejudice?"

Ellie shrugged. "Maybe you're right. I'm still jumpy about Brian—about men in general, I guess."

"Look, even if you're wrong about what you saw in there tonight, it doesn't make any difference to me."

Was Mac telling her the truth? She probed his warm, dark eyes. A yearning started, low and deep within her, and it caught Ellie by surprise.

Mac tried to remain patient. "How about it? I'll trade you a ride in my jet for what you did for me tonight?"

"Is that just another form of a date?"

Mac grinned. "Maybe it is."

She felt heat climb into her cheeks. "If I didn't know any better, Major Stanford, I'd say you're an ace at handing out lines."

"Thank you, ma'am. So, will you fly with me?"

How could she say no? Ellie murmured, "All right."

"Great." Mac felt ten pounds drop off his shoulders. As he watched Ellie sit down and arrange the folds of her white cotton skirt, he was again drawn to her simple honesty, the way she lived her life. Shutting the door, he dug the keys out of his pocket, whistling softly. Tomorrow he'd drop over to the provost marshal's office, and then he'd arrange a flight for this lady who had the warmth of the earth in her.

Mac picked up the phone in his office. It was nearly 1700, quitting time for the day. Glancing out his window toward Hangar 13, he dialed Ellie's number.

"Hello?"

"Ellie, this is Mac."

"Hi."

He smiled and relaxed back into his chair. Cradling the phone between his ear and his shoulder, he said, "I thought you'd like to know that I was over at the provost marshal's office this morning."

"Really? What did you find out?"

He heard the wariness in her voice. "Nothing yet. But an interesting fact came up. Five years ago a Sergeant Tim Olson disappeared from the base. At first, he was considered AWOL, but they left the case open, because Olson never showed up at his home in Nebraska, or anywhere else."

"Why would you pinpoint Olson?"

"An interesting coincidence, Ellie. Olson used to work in a small building on the very site that Hangar 13 was later built upon."

"Oh..."

"What do you think?"

"Well, could Olson have been murdered here where the hangar was built?"

"You tell me."

"I really don't know. The spirit wouldn't give his name."

Mac sat up straight. "I think it's an interesting piece of evidence.... How are you doing today?"

"Fine. I've done four journeys for clients and I'm getting ready to call it quits for the day."

He smiled, liking Ellie's laughter. "How would you like to meet for dinner? There's a nice little Italian restaurant about halfway between your home and mine. What do you say?" Mac held his breath, hoping she would finally say yes.

"I can't, Mac. I'm sorry, I have a speaking engagement tonight. . . ."

He heard the apology in her tone. "If you didn't have this talk, would you have said yes?" he teased.

"I don't think you take no for an answer, Major Stanford."

With a smile, he said, "You're right."

"Is this kind of behavior intrinsic to military men? Or just you?"

It was his turn to laugh. Mac had missed Ellie acutely throughout the day. He had known her just a few days, but already she seemed an integral part of his life. "I think it's kind of endemic with our breed, Ms. O'Gentry. Once you get to know us, though, we're not a bad lot."

"That's your viewpoint, Major. I think I'd like a second opinion."

"You can have one. Just say you'll go to dinner with me sometime this coming week."

"I think you should have been an attorney."

"Is that a yes?"

"Maybe . . ."

He flipped open his appointment book. "Mark down May 15."

"Why?"

"That's when you get to fly with me."

"Really?"

Mac liked the excitement he heard in her voice. "That's a roger."

"What time?"

"Oh-seven hundred. We'll fly in the early morning when the air is smoother. I don't want you getting airsick on me."

With a laugh, Ellie said, "Okay, May 15. I'll be there."

"Good." Mac felt the tension draining out of him. "Listen, getting serious here for a minute, I'm going to snoop around some more on this Olson angle."

"Even if you don't believe in ghosts?"

"Yes." He shrugged. "I've been thinking a lot about you, Ellie, about your beliefs. And I remembered when I was a kid, I would get these thoughts. A few minutes later, my mother would say what I'd just thought."

"Mental telepathy. I'm impressed."

"You ought to be. The point is, I've been racking my brain for other instances of mysterious, unexplained behavior."

"Besides something throwing wrenches at your people and a screwdriver at me."

He liked her ability to tease; Ellie gave as well as she got. "I think I had that coming. I'm willing to concede that there are some unexplained phenomena in this world."

"My heart be still!"

Mac laughed. He didn't want to get off the phone, but he had to. "If I find anything more on Olson, I'll give you a call."

"Okay, but Mac?"

"Yes?"

"Just be careful in that corner of the hangar."

"I've already rearranged the work areas in the hangar. That corner is now liberated from any activity." He grimaced, glancing out onto the floor of the hangar, where several crews were working on the jets. "We're a little crowded in this end, and my people are grumbling about the tight quarters, but I don't care."

"Have any of them guessed what is happening?"

"No, only my master sergeant. He knows I've contacted you, but we haven't discussed it."

"I think I should try to journey again and see if I can get some more information from the spirit. Maybe if we tell him we know about Tim Olson, that might help. He was acting as if he expected me to know a lot more than I did."

"Then," Mac said lightly, "I'll do some more snooping around at the PM's office and see what I can find."

CHAPTER SIX

Ellie tried to still her excitement as she waited at the visitor's entrance of Luke Air Force Base. She had worn pale green slacks, comfortable tennis shoes and a white blouse. Mac had told her to wear pants because of all the gear she'd have to don. She stood at the window that overlooked the main base area. Even at seven in the morning, it was busy with vehicles and personnel, and jets taking off. There was always the growl and vibration of jets in the background, and it thrilled Ellie, although she couldn't have said why.

Her heart pounded a bit harder in her breast when she saw Mac drive up and park next to the building. She hadn't seen him in nearly two weeks, and it seemed like forever. How handsome and self-assured he looked in his olive green flight suit, with the dark blue, silver-trimmed cap cocked on his head at a rakish angle. There was nothing not to like about Mac Stanford, Ellie decided. She realized with a start that her palms were damp. Damp, of all things! At her age, she'd thought such reactions to a man were things of the past. But not with Mac.

She tried to look composed as she watched him walk confidently toward the door. His hair was dark and gleaming, and his face was free of that dark beard that always seem to shadow his features in the late afternoon. As he drew closer, Ellie swore she could see gold sunlight dancing in his hazel eyes. More than anything, she liked his hands. They were long and strong looking, almost artistic in appearance, save for the large, rawboned knuckles. Mac possessed strong hands, and more than once, Ellie wondered almost foolishly what it would be like to have them caressing her shoulders.

She had tried to keep Mac at bay within her heart—but it was almost impossible. She thought of him constantly while she was working, and his face would appear every night when she was getting ready for bed. Mac made her heart pound and her pulse flutter; like a rare, beautiful perfume, he had scented her life in a way no man had ever done before.

As Mac entered the visitor's office, he automatically took off his cap and turned in her direction. His smile was blinding, filled with undeniable welcome, and Ellie felt his warmth envelop her. She felt heat nettling her cheeks and groaned to herself. She was blushing! Without thinking, she touched her left cheek as Mac approached. How could she have denied him dinner these past weeks? It was crazy to keep turning him down, Ellie's heart told her. But her head was always lurking in the background, whispering to her to be careful.

"Hi, stranger," Mac said in greeting. He held out his hand toward her as he closed the distance between them. How beautiful and simple Ellie looked amidst all the hustle and bustle of the base. Her white blouse had long shirttails that swept across her hips and emphasized the rounded curves of her body. Her hair was pinned up and tamed in a bun at the nape of her neck. What a shame, Mac thought, as he saw her shy smile. Never had he been so intrigued with a woman's hair. He longed to ease his fingers through it, feel its sleekness, bury his face in it.

"Hi..." Ellie said awkwardly as she slipped her hand into his. Mac's hand was dry and warm. As his fingers folded gently around hers, Ellie felt a frisson of heat fly up her arm. Her heart beat dangerously fast as he halted only inches from her. Being around Mac was like being around Father Sun, Ellie decided, as she was gently snared by his dancing eyes. His mouth was curved with genuine pleasure, and she wondered abstractly what it would be like to kiss that mouth. There was such strength and power surrounding him. Did he realize it? Ellie didn't think so.

"Well, are you ready to become an eagle today?" he teased. He was determined to keep things light. But his wild, almost insatiable urge to sweep Ellie into his arms and feel her ripely curved body against his was nearly his undoing. When he took a step back, he saw the relief in Ellie's warm brown eyes. He saw fear there, too. He supposed it would take more time to gain her trust. But he intended to do it. In the two weeks they'd been apart, Mac had realized that he wanted to know Ellie better, no matter what their differences.

Ellie laughed a little and noticed that a number of the uniformed air police were discreetly watching them. She felt uncomfortable. "Yes, I guess I am."

Mac reached out and touched her upper arm. "Come on, I'll take you over to our fitting facility. My crew is finishing up a check on my bird. As soon as they're done, we'll be off."

Mac's touch sent a sizzling, almost painful sense of need throughout Ellie. She felt it deep within her. How long had she gone without a man in her life? Far too long. That ache, that unfulfilled feeling, had surfaced now and then, but never like this. Never had she felt this sharp, clamoring longing that Mac always set off within her.

When they reached the parking lot, Mac opened the door to the car and she got in. The sun had heated the vehicle considerably, but Ellie loved the sun and luxuriated in the warmth.

When Mac got in, he turned and smiled at her. "In two weeks, you've become prettier than ever."

She lowered her lashes and avoided his burning gaze, the message in which was easily translated: he wanted her. The thought was as exciting as it was forbidden to Ellie. Clasping her hands in her lap, she murmured, "Thank you."

Mac drove his car down one boulevard and turned onto another. Driving on base was always slow business. Though he kept his eyes on the road, he could sense Ellie's discomfort and wondered if it was specifically him—or if it would be the same with any man who showed an interest in her. He wished he had the guts to ask her exactly that, but he felt such a tentative, almost fragile bond between them, and didn't want to destroy what was already in place.

Maybe, if she got to know him better, she'd lose the wariness that stood like a wall between them. He gestured toward the flight line in the distance.

"My crew thinks you're a public-relations ride. I'm letting them think that, because we usually don't give civilians a ride in our jets."

"I'm scared and excited, if you want the truth."

"About being around me or taking a hop?" The words came out before Mac could stop them.

Ellie met his eyes, and again, her pulse bounded. She didn't know how to answer him.

"I'm sorry," Mac said. "I know you don't trust me. I wish you did, that's all."

She felt his pain, but she also sensed that Mac understood why she held him off. "If I didn't trust you, Major, I wouldn't be flying in that jet of yours."

His grin broadened a little. "Really?" His hopes rose.

"Really."

After that, the tension seemed to lessen between them, and Mac filled Ellie in on his progress with Hangar 13. "It took me a while, but I finally managed to find out where Tim Olson's parents live. I gave them a call."

"Oh?"

"Tim never showed up at home," Mac said. He turned down another street, which led toward the flight line. "I talked to his mother, who thinks that her son was murdered. She said Tim liked the military, that being in the air force had been his life's dream."

"It wouldn't make sense that he'd go AWOL then, would it?"

With a shake of his head, Mac said, "No, it wouldn't. Mrs. Olson was very nice to me. I asked her if Tim had any enemies and she said he had none."

"What was he like?" Ellie asked.

"I asked her about that, too. Tim was a fairly aggressive man. He played sports in high school, was real competitive and didn't like to lose."

"That fits," Ellie said. "The spirit was very aggressive. Did Mrs. Olson say anything about her son having a temper? That spirit was very angry."

"I remember that," Mac said. He pulled up to a single-story building and shut off the engine. "She told me that Tim had temper tantrums as a kid. And in high school, whenever he lost a game, he would throw things in the locker room."

Ellie's eyes widened. She saw how serious Mac had become. "This spirit is throwing things, too."

"Yes." He fought the desire to brush his hand through Ellie's black, thick hair. "I've had two weeks to think about what you saw in your journey, and I'm still not convinced. But Tim Olson seems to match the temperament of the spirit you saw and spoke to."

Ellie felt him wrestling with the situation. Without thinking, she reached out and placed her hand on his sleeve. "It's very hard to make the leap of faith it takes to accept what I do, what I believe in and what I see when I'm in an altered state, Mac." She removed her hand, although she wanted to continue exploring the steel-cable muscles of his arm. She saw Mac's eyes suddenly become narrowed, filled with heat, with desire—for her. She quickly added, "Don't try to force yourself to believe any of it. That's not being true to yourself. You don't have to believe on my account. Remember? I'm used to naysayers." She lifted her arm and gestured outside the car. "The world is filled with them."

A slight smile tugged at Mac's mouth as he opened the car door. "I'm not trying to force myself to believe anything, Ellie." He gave her a long, serious look. "But facts are facts. The description you gave me of the spirit's personality seems to match Tim Olson's almost exactly. You may think I have a fairly rigid outlook on life, but I'm not one to disagree with facts. Fair enough?"

She met his smile and felt surrounded with that wonderful heat once again. "Fair enough," she murmured, nervous beneath his hooded look.

"Come on," he said, excitement in his voice, "let's get you a pair of g-chaps, a helmet and some flight boots, and we'll be off."

For the next hour, Ellie was the center of attention. Two sergeants in charge of flight gear fitted her with a form-hugging, lower-body g-suit that was designed to stop the blood from leaving her head in high-g turns. They fussed over her, helped tighten the g-chaps to fit her legs, and found a pair of heavy black leather flight boots in her size.

When they were finished, Ellie couldn't help but laugh. Beneath her left arm was a helmet and oxygen mask. "I feel like a trussed-up goose that's ready to be roasted!"

Everyone laughed. Mac grinned and gestured for her to follow him. "Believe me, when you get up in the jet, you'll be glad for those g-chaps fitting so tightly. Let's go. Our steed awaits."

A thrill filled Ellie as she followed Mac back out to the car. It was eight a.m., and the light blue sky was filled with the blinding radiance of the sun. The slight chill of earlier was gone, replaced with that dry warmth she loved so much. Getting into the car, Ellie felt anticipation thrumming through her.

"I don't know if I'm more scared or excited," she confided to Mac.

"A healthy combination."

"You aren't going to make me airsick, are you?"

"No." He turned and met her large, luminous eyes. A man could lose his soul in them, he decided, then pushed the thought aside. "I want you to understand what I do, why I enjoy it so much."

Ellie nodded. "You're much more subtle than I gave you credit for."

"What do you mean?"

It was her turn to smile. "If I understand you, the man, you're thinking maybe I won't be as gun-shy around you."

"Guilty," Mac conceded. He pulled onto a road that would lead them directly to his jet waiting outside Hangar 13. "I know your ex-husband didn't believe in you." He gestured to the jet in the distance. "I can't fight city hall. I need you to see for yourself that I'm different. Maybe if you set foot in my world for a while, you won't be so scared of me."

Ellie colored fiercely over his honesty. "I feel badly, but I can't apologize, Mac."

"No one's asking you to." He pulled the car up beside the hangar and put it in park. Taking out the key, he turned and held her sad eyes. "I know I was pretty skeptical of you, what you do, at first."

"And now?"

Mac felt the tension in her and wished he could make it go away. "Now, it's not so farfetched as it seemed before." He shrugged and reached over and captured her hand. He squeezed her fingers and then released them. "Maybe," he hedged, "with time and education both ways, we'll be able to see each other, not what we do for a living."

Ellie's hand tingled. She sat there, feeling a tidal wave of joy combined with warning. "Mac, what you do for a living isn't necessarily tied to your beliefs the way it is for me."

"Yes, it is," he murmured. "Ellie, I'm in the military because I believe in the defense of our country. I don't *like* war, I don't like the thought of killing another human being, but I do believe that our people should be free, and I'm willing to fight for that right. So what I do for a living is as much a part of my belief system as shamanism is of yours."

A lot of different, difficult emotions played through Ellie as she digested his words. "I—I guess—" she stumbled, searching for the right words "—I've got a lot of prejudice, too, in a sense."

Mac sat back. "How so?"

With a painful shrug, Ellie whispered, "I'm so used to people outside my world pooh-poohing what I do, what I believe in, that I'm tired of defending it. So many have called me crazy that I assume everyone in the so-called real world feels that way." She searched his face and saw understanding burning in the depths of his eyes, and it gave her the courage to go on. Opening her hands, she said, "Mac, we live in a society that doesn't believe in the unseen, the metaphysics of life. I spent many years trying to get people to consider another point of view. But even my husband, the man I was supposedly closest to, couldn't accept it. Brian was always calling me crazy. It hurt a lot. After a while, it got so bad I never said anything to him about my world, my profession. It was okay for him to tell me about his work, his problems with certain people, the pressures on him, but he never wanted to hear them from me."

"You had a one-way relationship," Mac agreed quietly.

"It was more than that. I literally felt like a ghost in our household. As long as I fit the 'normal' mode of housewife—cooking, sewing, cleaning—then things were fine between us. But if I ever brought up the things that really mattered to me..." She grimaced. "Every time I did, it meant an argument, yelling. I hate fighting, Mac. I cringe just thinking about it."

"You're a gentle person."

Shaken by his insight into her, Ellie raised her chin sharply and looked at him. Mac's eyes were touched with pain—and she realized it was her pain. Never had she encountered a man who could feel so much for anyone outside of himself. "Y-yes, I'm gentle in the sense that, because of my abilities, I can't tolerate the normal stresses this society puts on us." With a sigh, she added, "That's why I have a small house near the edge of the city. I need the earth nearby, not the noise, the hustle or the frantic energy that city life provides. I've always found peace in my garden."

"But not in people?"

His insight stunned her. Ellie swallowed convulsively. "How can you see through me so easily?"

"I'm a pilot as a profession, a human being all the time, Ellie."

She knew he didn't mean that as a barb. Hanging her head, she whispered, "I'm afraid of you, Mac. Actually, I'm more afraid of myself. You scare me because you make me feel emotions I've never felt. You give me hope, but I'm too scared to reach out and take it."

Gently, he picked up her hand and placed it between his own. The jet ride could wait. This was more important. "Look," Mac began huskily, "let the time we spend together talk to you, Ellie. I know we all put up walls, we project on other people, on situations. When you look at me, your brain says 'Brian.'" He smiled a little, a catch in his voice. "What I keep hoping is that your heart sees *me.*"

Closing her eyes, Ellie felt tears begin to form. "You're an eagle. I'm a dove."

"Can a bird of war get along with a bird of peace?" Mac posed softly. He patted her hand and allowed her to reclaim it. As she opened her eyes, he saw the tears in them. Without a word, he pulled a white handkerchief from the side pocket of his flight suit and handed it to her. He hoped the tears symbolized something good between them, not something negative. After blotting her eyes, she refolded the handkerchief and gave it back to him. Without a word, he stuffed it away and zipped the pocket up again.

"Come on, let's fly," he whispered, and opened the door of the car.

Ellie perked up as Mac's enthusiastic crew surrounded them at the base of the ladders to the huge, gleaming jet. She was in awe of the power that surrounded the aircraft, and now understood a little better why Mac had that same power around him. It were as if two giants with equal strength, intelligence and competitiveness had met. Who would be the eventual winner? It had to be Mac, she surmised as she climbed carefully up the aluminium ladder to the rear cockpit seat. His world was one of metal, instruments and cold, hard reality. What he saw on the instrument panel before him was everything—his life or his death.

After she was strapped into the harness system and the helmet had been settled on her head, Ellie watched with fascination as Mac climbed up the ladder and moved into the front cockpit. He was all-business, and so was his crew. She sat in the hot sun, sweat beginning to form on her brow. She couldn't remember ever feeling more confined.

As the ladders were withdrawn from the sleek aircraft, Ellie saw the crew chief give a signal with her hands. Mac acknowledged the signal, and suddenly the entire jet began to tremble. The quivering reminded Ellie of a horse she had grown up with on the reservation, an old thoroughbred who had outlasted his usefulness on the race track, but had never forgotten how to run. Every time she'd thrown her bare leg across his narrow, ridged back, she'd felt the very same quiver—one of anticipation mingled with excitement.

The huge Plexiglas canopy slowly came down over them. A rasping sound came through the headset within the helmet, and then Ellie heard Mac's voice.

"We're on intercabin frequency as well as with my crew chief," he told her briskly. "Right now I'm running through a final check of all my instruments and making sure both engines are in good shape. How you doing back there?"

She smiled nervously. "Okay, I guess. I was thinking this jet was like a thoroughbred gelding I used to ride when I was growing up. He always quivered when he wanted to run."

Mac's laugh was husky. "Yep, this girl of mine likes to run, too."

"You call this plane a girl?"

Chuckling, Mac looked up and snapped a sharp salute to his crew chief. "Listen, when a plane has this much power, it's gotta be a woman."

"On that we agree." Ellie laughed. Her excitement doubled as the engines began to whine higher and louder, although the sound was somewhat muted by the helmet she wore. Still, she could feel the power, the trembling, through every pore, bone and muscle in her body.

"Okay, let's stroll on out to the takeoff point," he told her.

Ellie felt the engines begin a deeper growl, felt the jet gently begin to move forward. It gave her a euphoric sense of power, with none of the foreboding she'd thought would accompany it. From the ground, the jet had looked predatory. Riding *in* it gave her an altogether different outlook. She felt as if she was master over a very powerful piece of machinery.

At the ramp, another vehicle came up and several men got out.

"Put your hands up on the edge of the cockpit. Those fellows are the armorers, and they're going to check beneath the wings of the jet. They want to see our hands, because that means we won't accidentally run over them."

There was amusement in Mac's voice, but she knew he was serious. She saw him place both hands at the top of aircraft frame, in plain sight. As soon as she did the same, the three crewmen disappeared beneath their plane for the inspection.

"You aren't carrying any weapons, are you?"

"No, but we always go through this drill. How you doing back there?"

"Fine. Excited. Scared."

"I feel the excitement every time I sit in this hot seat up here."

"I can see why you love to fly. This plane is awesome."

Chuckling, Mac nodded. "Welcome to my world, Ms. O'Gentry."

"Your world is something else." She saw the three air crewmen reappear and move back to their vehicle. One saluted, and she saw Mac snap a return salute.

"Okay, we're ready to roll. Your harness good and tight?"

"So tight I feel like my blood supply is cut off," Ellie complained.

"You won't feel that way after we take off, believe me," he replied dryly.

Ellie heard the engines growl again, and once more, he eased the huge jet forward. All around her was desert; cactus, chaparral and sandy soil surrounded the long, black runway. She looked up through the Plexiglas canopy and saw how light the sky was. Far above them were horsetail-cirrus clouds, long, fine and filmy. It was a beautiful morning.

"Ready for takeoff?" Mac asked her, settling both feet hard on the rudders to make the jet stop as he started to ease both throttles forward.

"Yes."

He smiled to himself as he heard the excitement in her voice. "Okay, we're going to make an afterburner's takeoff. At the end of the runway, I'm going to stand this girl on her tail and we're going to go straight up for thirty thousand feet. This is called grandstanding. It impresses everyone." He chuckled. "You're going to feel a lot of pressure on your body—that's just gravity. So relax, let it push you into the seat and enjoy the ride."

Ellie nodded tensely. Her heart was pumping hard. "Okay," she whispered. Mac didn't have to tell her what to expect, but he had, and she was grateful. In her right hand, she clutched the airsick bag.

"Your oxygen mask strapped on?" Mac asked as he began to inch the throttles toward the afterburner range.

"Yes."

"Good. Okay, we've got clearance. Here we go— the eagle and the dove together."

Ellie didn't have time to respond to his words. The instant Mac released the rudders, she was slammed hard against the seat. Her breath was squeezed out of her as the engines roared, caught and moved into the afterburner range. The ground was moving so fast that it made her dizzy. The pressure on her body increased as the jet raced down the runway. Somewhere in her spinning thoughts, she knew Mac loved this. The jet was like an unleashed cougar running down the airstrip, howling and snarling.

Ellie gasped loudly as, at the end of the runway, Mac suddenly brought the jet into a ninety-degree turn, and they were heading straight up toward the sky. She could barely catch her breath, the pressure was so intense. The throbbing, pounding pulse of the jet engines converged in a rhythmic unison that seemed to permeate her soul. Shutting her eyes tightly, Ellie could feel the sensations, the pressure, the pain in her thighs as the g-chaps inflated tight and hard against her lower extremities. She opened her eyes slightly and saw the light blue sky was getting darker.

"Ten thousand," Mac told her.

Ellie heard the strain in his voice. Yet he seemed alert. Her brain felt fuzzy, and her eyesight was graying.

"Fifteen."

The pressure increased on her entire body and Ellie could barely move her fingers. She felt crushed against the seat, as if a huge, invisible hand was pressing down on her. Her eyes felt as if they were being pushed back through the rear of her skull. The oxygen mask bit sharply into the flesh across the bridge of her nose.

"Twenty."

Gasping, she tried to breathe. She heard Mac grunting through the headset and remembered belatedly that she should be doing the same thing. The grunting brought oxygen back into the body.

"Twenty-five."

Ellie felt like a puppet whose strings belonged to someone else. She could only lie flattened against the seat, gasping, trying to hold on to consciousness.

"Leveling out at thirty...."

Suddenly, the gravity, the crush, began to release her. Ellie's vision cleared remarkably swiftly as Mac brought the jet into level flight. To her amazement, the sky up here was a dark, cobalt blue. They were flying within filmy cirrus clouds. The view was awe inspiring, and Ellie gasped again—this time not for oxygen, but for the overwhelming beauty surrounding them.

"Quite a sight, isn't it?" Mac asked.

Shaken, Ellie wondered if he'd read her thoughts. Breathing through the oxygen mask was demanding, but she managed to find her voice and said, "I never realized how beautiful it was up here."

"Most don't, or we'd all be pilots." Mac chuckled indulgently. He lifted his gloved hand and pointed upward. "If you go to forty thousand, the sky becomes almost like night. It reminds me of a dark blue sapphire. It's breathtaking."

"Y-yes, it's all breathtaking."

"You doing okay?"

"I think so...."

"What did you think of the gravity?"

"Awful!"

Mac laughed. "Yeah, it's a dog, all right. How did you like elevator flight? Pretty impressive, huh?"

Mac was like a little boy sharing his favorite marbles with her, Ellie thought. She could hear the joy in his voice. "It was something else," she agreed. "It was uncomfortable."

"After a while, it gets to be one hell of a joyride," Mac told her enthusiastically as he banked the jet to the left. "It's like riding an exploding cannon, only you're strapped onto the front of it."

Laughing a little, Ellie said, "I think you're right, but I still feel like I'm not fully in my body yet."

"A little like being in an altered state?"

"How could you know?"

"Flying's a little like your journeying, I think. When the blood leaves my head on tight turns or afterburner stage, I don't feel very much in my body, either. In fact, it's a struggle to stay in it. With all the blood draining from my brain, I want to lose consciousness."

"I'm impressed," Ellie said simply, "with your insight. But when I journey, Mac, the blood doesn't leave my head."

"I know that. But I think the feeling may be the same."

"It is." She was humbled by his struggle to understand her and her world in the context of his own.

"You're awful quiet back there," he said after five minutes of silence.

"I was thinking," Ellie admitted.

"Yes?"

"About you." She looked around through the clear canopy, once again struck by the ephemeral beauty of the sky that embraced them. "You love flying because it gives you a sense of freedom."

"Actually," Mac drawled, "a release."

"From what?"

"Life down on the ground. Up here there are no hassles, no managerial problems facing me—"

"No wrenches thrown through the air?"

He laughed deep and long. "Bingo. You got it."

"How do you feel after you land?"

"Like I want to climb right back and take off again."

"Why?"

"I don't know," Mac admitted thoughtfully, glancing around, always on the lookout for other aircraft. He pointed the jet toward Flagstaff, a good one hundred miles away. "I can think better up here. I have clarity, I guess. I can have a headache at the office, but if I fly on that day, the headache goes away."

"That's a little what journeying is like for me," Ellie told him. Below, she could see the desert and small, green shapes she assumed to be cactus. "When I'm in that altered state, I feel lighter, freer."

"Do you like coming back?"

"I don't mind it. But then, I don't journey to escape, Mac. Do you fly to escape?"

He chuckled. "Sometimes I do—I have to admit it. Being up here makes me feel better. When you come back from a journey, do you feel better?"

"Every time. It's a very energizing, vital thing to me, and I always feel better when I come back. There have been times I've had to journey when I wasn't feeling very well. Afterward, I always feel wonderful."

"So do I. See? We aren't as different as you might think."

Touched, Ellie said nothing. Ahead, she could see what looked like a nap over the curved surface of the earth, and she was sure it was forest. "Where are you taking us?"

"I thought we'd tour Flag and look at the red rocks of Sedona, then go home. I've got an hour of flight time, and I want to use all of it."

Smiling, Ellie truly began to relax. The pressures were no longer on her body, and she was able to breathe without trouble. "I can see why you like your world. It's a beautiful one."

"Up here," Mac agreed, "everything looks good. Up here I don't see the violence, the pollution, or hear the bad news from around the world."

"It's a very safe place," Ellie agreed.

"In one way. Right now you're getting the nickel tour, with no jet acrobatics or the type of flying I usually do when I'm training for dogfights."

"Oh?"

"Yeah, it's usually a lot more violent, a lot more physically demanding."

"As brutal as that vertical climb?"

"The same, sometimes worse."

Ellie shook her head. "I don't know how you do it."

"Believe me, flying these jets is for young bodies only. I'm reaching the upper limits of my flying, agewise. I don't take the g's as well as I used to, and I'm taking vitamin A to keep my night vision top-notch."

"You mean you'll have to stop flying?"

"Eventually, they'll ground me to a complete desk job and I'll be allowed only so many flight hours a month. I'll fly a desk, not a plane."

Ellie heard the sadness in his voice. "I don't know how I'd feel if my ability to journey was taken away from me."

"It's not a day I'm looking forward to, believe me. I've thought about resigning and flying commercial planes. That way, I can continue to fly, at least until I'm sixty."

"But no afterburners, no vertical climbs," Ellie noted.

"No," Mac said, "but I'm an eagle, remember? I don't want my wings clipped. I don't want to be grounded for the rest of my life. Flying's in my blood, like journeying is in yours. Maybe it's genetic. Who knows? If I don't get at least fifteen hours of flying a month, I'm a bastard to be around."

Ellie laughed. "Well, I don't have that kind of mood turn if I don't journey."

"How many a month do you do?"

"I do up to four a day. That's all I can tolerate without becoming completely ungrounded or feeling spacey all the time."

"Four journeys for four different people?"

"Yes."

"You usually do them in the morning?"

"Shamans vary," Ellie told him as she watched the dark green carpet of forest beneath them. To the left, she could see the red sandstone formations surrounding Sedona. "I was taught to do my journeying when I was at my strongest point. For me, that's the morning. That's when my energy is at its peak."

"I've been trying to understand what you do," Mac said, banking the plane to the left to take in the redrock view. "You have to have a tremendous amount of concentration and focus, just like I do when I fly a plane."

"That's right," Ellie said. She smiled softly. "Why do I get the feeling you're trying to find every possible parallel between flying and journeying you can?"

"Because," Mac said dryly, "I'm trying to get you to see that we're not so different, after all."

"You do it physically. I do mine mentally."

"So what?"

Ellie wrestled with his challenge. "It's not that easy to make a comparison, Mac."

"I think it is."

"That's because you *want* to find similarities."

"Anything wrong with that?"

Ellie tried to concentrate on the beauty of the sandstone formations below them. At this altitude she could see the entire area. She knew from talking to local Navajo and Hopi medicine people that the Sedona area was considered highly sacred, a woman's area; even to this day, ceremonies were performed there.

"Cat got your tongue?" Mac teased as he turned the jet back toward Phoenix.

"No...."

"I've been giving a lot of thought to what you said earlier about mental telepathy."

"Oh?"

"I guess I have my share of it," Mac admitted. "Before meeting you, I just wasn't tuned in to that portion of myself."

"All humans have the capacity for mental telepathy."

"I won't disagree. One time my crew chief, Sergeant Susan Greer, had this hunch that something was wrong with one of the engines on this jet. It was just a feeling. I was supposed to fly that morning, but she asked me to scrub the mission in order to check out the engine. I was a little uptight about it, because with my schedule, flying time isn't always easily arranged, but I trusted her." Mac chuckled. "Wouldn't you know, Susan found that one of the blades in the engine had a nice big fracture through it. If I'd disregarded her hunch and flown, that engine piece would have loosened and ended up tearing the hell out of the rest of it and probably exploding."

A chill ran down Ellie's back. "That's terrible!"

"It could have been," Mac told her blithely, "but my gut told me to listen to Susan and trust her judgment. I'm glad I did." He began to ease the jet down from thirty thousand, only this time, he did it more gradually, so that it was comfortable for Ellie. "I've been remembering a lot of incidents like that over the last two weeks."

"Humans sometimes work out of the right brain without ever knowing it."

"I believe that now. I do. I have to admit I was skeptical at first, but the more we talked, and the more I thought about it, the more sense it all made."

If only Brian could have gleaned such wisdom from his life and applied it to hers! Ellie shook her head. She saw the last of the forest carpet fade away and the gold-and-red sand begin. For some reason, she didn't want this flight to end.

"When we get back, I'd like to take you to the O Club on base for breakfast. We'll land at 0930. What do you say?"

Her stomach was growling. Ellie wondered if he could hear it through his headset and then laughed at herself. Of course he couldn't! Mac had warned her not to eat any breakfast, to reduce the chance of airsickness.

"I am hungry."

"Okay. The Officers Club is a nice place. They serve up a mean chili omelet."

"Chili? This time of morning?"

Laughing, Mac said, "I like hot food. When I got assigned to Luke last year, I was in seventh heaven with all the Mexican food. Salsa, hot sauce and red-hot peppers are my favorites."

"You're a lot braver than I am." Ellie laughed. "Thanks, but I think I'll settle for a very bland plate of scrambled eggs and bacon."

"Anything the lady wants," Mac drawled.

Ellie was a little shaky after climbing out of all the gear. Mac smiled understandingly, put his hand beneath her elbow and led her out into the bright, hot sunlight.

"I feel reborn," Ellie said.

"How so?" He opened her car door.

"I just feel cleaner, as if somehow flying cleansed my aura. I get a similar sensation when I swim or take a shower." Ellie climbed in and buckled the seat belt.

Mac was happier than he could ever recall. He climbed into the car and placed the key into the ignition. Glancing over at Ellie, whose cheeks were flaming red, he said, "Flying is like a hot shower to me, too." But about now he could use a cold shower. Every little movement Ellie made entranced him. He simply couldn't get enough of her. There was such a vibrant look to her golden eyes, to the soft curve of her lips. And her hair... He groaned to himself and forced his attention to the road. Ellie's hair was in disarray, tendrils softening the natural angularity of her cheekbones. Mac found himself wanting to tame each errant strand back into place, the sensation electric and heated.

At the O Club, Mac asked for and got a booth in a quiet corner. Not many officers were in the club right now, since it was past breakfast and most of them were at work. He felt as if he was walking on clouds with Ellie at his side. After they were seated, he ordered them strong, black coffee. Folding his hands, he smiled across the table at her.

"You look a little like a fish out of water here," he observed.

Ellie opened her purse and pulled out her brush. "Wearing civilian clothes around here does make me stand out," she noted with a smile. She saw Mac's eyes grow hooded as she unpinned her hair and allowed it to tumble loose across her back and shoulders.

Mac tried to tame his reaction to Ellie's innocent action. Her hair, rich and abundant, flowed like a black river through her long, brown fingers, and he ached to reach out and touch those vibrant strands. Swallowing hard, he tried to focus on something else. He grabbed his coffee cup and took a quick gulp, nearly burning his mouth in the process.

Grasping for a safe topic, he decided to talk about his youth. "When I was a kid growing up in Oregon, I used to watch the bald eagles flying. I would sit on top of one of the sand dunes and watch those birds for hours. My mother used to accuse me of being a daydreamer. When I was seven I thought that if I wanted a pair of wings badly enough, they would replace my arms." He smiled sheepishly. "Crazy, huh?"

Touched, Ellie shook her head. "I was taught a long time ago that anything we really desire out of life, we can make come into reality. You wanted to be a bird, so the next best thing was to become a pilot. You might not have known it at the time, but out of your heart, your desire, you created a situation that fit into this third-dimensional reality. Your plane has wings."

Chuckling, he nodded. "When you were a little girl, did you want to grow up to be a shamaness?"

Ellie shook her head. "Not consciously."

"Subconsciously?"

"I must have or I wouldn't have created this reality I live in."

"Interesting philosophy," Mac said. "That whatever we desire can be ours."

"Up to a point, it's true," Ellie told him seriously, sipping her coffee. "I believe we have many lives, and before we go into a life, we choose what we want to learn in that lifetime. We may have to pay back some people, or give to others, plus try to learn what we've set out to master in this lifetime."

"That's called karma, right?"

"There's karma, which is what you owe others, and dharma, which is a gift you deserve. It's a give-and-take system."

"Give me an example." Mac liked her intelligence, her very different way of seeing the world.

"Well," Ellie said, "from a personal standpoint, I met Brian. He was highly prejudiced against me, against my beliefs. Unfortunately, I was young and naive, and I believed love could overcome such things. One time, I journeyed to find out why we had this standoff, and my spirit guide took me into a past life where Brian was a Puritan and I was a European landowner. I did not have any religious tolerance toward him, and I threw him off my land, along with his family of seven children. Four of them died of starvation, and eventually, he went to America." She shrugged. "You see, I wasn't very tolerant of his beliefs, so in this lifetime, I got paid back for being that way. I learned to be highly tolerant of whatever reality a person wants to have—whether spiritual, religious or otherwise. So Brian was a good teacher to me in that way."

"Turnabout is fair play with karma?"

"You could say that."

Mac frowned. "You said you went into a past life you'd had with Brian. Is that something else you do as a shamaness?"

"On occasion. I don't make a practice of it. In Brian's case, I was trying to retrieve any missing pieces of his soul so that he could be whole in this lifetime. I felt that if I was allowed to collect those missing parts of him, no matter where they were—in this life or some other—that our marriage could endure."

"What happened?"

"I was able to recover the piece he'd lost in that past life and bring it back."

"Was he more tolerant of you then?"

With a sad smile, Ellie shook her head. "No, less."

The waitress came over and they gave their orders. Mac had a million questions to ask Ellie, but he tried not to appear too eager for fear of making her retreat once again.

"Is it common for a husband or wife to take pieces from each other?"

"Oh, yes," Ellie said, leaning back, her hands around the warm cup. "Even in the most positive of marriages, partners usually take from one another. They can't help themselves, sometimes, and it's usually done unconsciously."

"Can you give me an example?"

Ellie smiled at him. Mac was desperately trying to understand her world. The discovery touched her deeply, and yet she wasn't sure *why* he was so interested. Was he hoping she would drop her guard, so he could take advantage of her? No, her heart told her, he's sincere. Ellie would have been less scared if Mac had been like a couple of other men she'd known who had simply wanted her body. But he wasn't talking with her at length just for that—although she knew he was drawn to her. She could see the thoughtfulness in his dark, questioning eyes, and could hear it in the tenor of his deep voice. And she could see him struggling to put all this varied information together.

"I can cite my own marriage. I was so head over heels in love with Brian that I ignored his lack of tolerance. I thought I'd be excluded from that, but I was wrong. When I went on the first journey in his behalf, I found out I'd taken a piece of him, too. I was horrified that I'd done that, knowing what I do about the process. But, as my spirit guide explained to me, when we're needy, we take—whether it's right or wrong. We do it because we're human beings. Because we're imperfect."

"I must have a whole bunch of pieces of my ex-wife, Johanna," Mac said grimly.

"What makes you think so?" Ellie desperately wanted to know about him as a man, and how he was in relationships.

"I loved her and I didn't want the divorce," he said, taking a sip of coffee. "She accused me of loving flying more than her."

"Did you?"

"I...don't know." Mac shrugged almost painfully. "I was angry and upset with her when she accused me of that. I denied it. Later, when I got some distance on it, I could see her side of it. Anyway, I didn't want to lose Johanna, and I made it tough on her during the divorce hearing. I kept wanting us to try again, to try to patch it up. Eventually, she wore me down and I gave up. I got the message."

"That you loved your job more than her?"

"Yes. At least, that's the way she saw it."

"You probably have a couple of pieces of her," Ellie murmured.

Mac studied her for a long moment. "Could you give them back to her?"

She sat very still. "Are you asking me to do this out of your own curiosity about what I do, or are you asking because you care about Johanna?"

With a sigh, Mac said, "Both, to be honest."

"So, if I journey on your ex-wife's behalf, you want to test out what I do?"

"Yes, but only if it will help Johanna. She hasn't been well since the divorce, and I feel like I have something to do with that. Maybe I don't." He smiled sourly. "Maybe I'm crazy."

"No," Ellie said softly, "you aren't. Very frequently, when major pieces are taken from a person, they become ill. The more that's taken, the more chronic the condition."

"She contracted allergies after our divorce," he said unhappily, "and she's gone to a string of allergists. All they do is give her shots, and she's more miserable."

"Stress from a divorce is enough to make any immune system become depressed, and allergies could certainly develop as a result," Ellie said. "I'll journey for her, Mac, but understand I'll only help if I'm given permission to help her."

"Isn't my asking you to help enough?"

"No, because on that shamanistic level, I'm dealing with the lifelong karma of an individual. If I go in and 'fix' something that shouldn't be fixed—because the soul is supposed to learn from that situation in this lifetime—I'm in trouble. I can wind up with the karma that person was trying to work through, and I have no desire to handle any more than my own." Her mouth tugged into a grimace. "I have plenty."

The waitress came and delivered their breakfast orders. Mac thanked her and dug into his Mexican omelet. He saw Ellie roll her eyes.

"You must have a cast-iron stomach," she muttered as she cut into her own breakfast.

"I just like hot things."

"Yes," Ellie said, "hot cars, hot jets and probably hot women, not necessarily in that order."

Grinning, Mac said, "You cut me to the quick. It's true, I have a fast car—"

"And you fly a fast jet."

"My taste in women," he informed her, raising one eyebrow, "is different."

"Really?" Ellie wanted to ask him bluntly what kind of women he liked. She found it difficult to believe Mac was interested in her. He could probably have his pick of women—why would he single out someone so different from himself.

Mac knew what Ellie was implying, and he could see that her curiosity was getting the better of her. "What?" he asked. "You think I only date carbon copies of myself?"

"Not necessarily," Ellie hedged defensively.

"Actually, Johanna was a bit like you," he said dryly. "She liked gardening and was on the quiet side." But that was where the similarities ended. Johanna constantly worried about her weight; Ellie did not. Johanna was tall and modellike; Ellie was shorter and wonderfully rounded in all the right places. Johanna had always been extremely dependent; Ellie had a full, happy life of her own. "But," he teased, taking another bite of omelet, "Johanna had short hair and I like long hair. Very long, dark hair..."

Blushing, Ellie avoided his dancing, amused look. "Well," she whispered, spearing at her eggs, "let's just stick to the business at hand, Major. I'll do a journey for your wife today, when I get home. I'll call you tomorrow morning with the results. Fair enough?"

"Fair enough," Mac murmured, wanting to reach out and touch her flaming cheek. There was no pretense with Ellie, and he found that admirable. She made no apologies for who she was and what she felt.

Mac was at his office at 0730 the next morning. Most of the air force would be starting work at 0800. His office door was shut and he was catching up on some paperwork when his phone rang.

"Major Stanford," he answered.

"Mac? It's Ellie."

He smiled and sat back in his chair. "Good morning." Yesterday, after they'd shared breakfast at the O Club, Mac had wanted to kiss her goodbye, but his head and his heart had warned him not to overstep his bounds with her. At least, not yet. But she'd been in his thoughts ever since.

"You sound chipper this morning," Ellie said, a smile in her voice.

"I am, as a matter of fact."

"Is that a normal condition for you at this hour?"

"Not exactly." He gripped his mug of coffee and took a sip. "Usually, for the first hour I'm a bear, and no one dares talk to me. I need three cups of coffee to wake up. This morning, I bounded out of bed at 0600 and was at the office working an hour later."

"Sounds as if my journey worked. I received permission to get pieces for you as well as Johanna."

"Oh?" He sat up, suddenly at full attention. "What exactly happened?"

"When I went into the journey, my guide told me you both had pieces of each other, which is normal. He gave me permission to help both of you. I'll tell you what I saw, if you'd like."

"Sure, go ahead." Curiosity was eating Mac up. He had attributed his atypical burst of energy this morning to the time he'd spent with Ellie. Could there possibly be a more mystical explanation?

"The first place I went was the real world. You see, in the journeying mode, there are three places I can go—the light world, the real world and the dark world. These are just names for various dimensions, so don't get hung up on the wording. It's just how I perceive them when I'm in an altered state."

"So far, so good."

"My guide took me to a house. I saw you and Johanna in the kitchen, and you were arguing with each other. I want to describe her to you because it will help me double-check my own work."

"Okay . . ."

"The woman was about five feet ten inches tall and was built like a stick."

Mac chuckled. "Johanna is six feet tall and weighs exactly one hundred and thirty pounds. I guess you might call that a stick."

"She had short red hair and a lot of freckles across her nose and cheeks."

Dumbfounded, Mac nodded. "Yes, that's right." He was amazed at her accuracy. Could something have really happened? How else could she know so much? "What else?" he urged.

"She has blue eyes, and at the time of your argument, she was wearing long, beaded earrings. They were gold."

"Johanna had a favorite pair of gold beaded earrings," Mac confirmed. "This is amazing."

"Let's just see if I'm correct about the rest," she warned him seriously. "I don't know what the fight was about, but I saw you coming at her—not attacking her, exactly, but you did grip her by the shoulders. She didn't like your manhandling her that way, and she pulled away and slapped you in the face."

Mac shook his head, the memory of that particular fight coming back to him.

"Mac? Are you still there?"

"Uh, yes. Go on, Ellie."

"Did it happen as I described it?"

"Yes," he said heavily. "It was the first—and only—time in our marriage that I ever laid a hand on her. The divorce hearing was the next day, and I was desperate. I had just come back from Desert Storm, and the divorce papers had been sent to me over in Saudi Arabia. I was going out of my mind. Johanna wouldn't talk to me on the phone the few times I could get to one, and she wouldn't answer my letters. So this was my only chance. I was trying to talk her into waiting for at least a couple of months before she went through with the divorce. I wanted her to give us— me—one more chance. I know I shouldn't have grabbed her. I guess I just lost it."

"I'm sorry," Ellie whispered. "I saw a piece of you split off when she slapped you, and that was the one I retrieved from her to give back to you."

Rubbing his brow, Mac said, "This is incredible. I never told anyone about that fight. Not anyone."

"And I'll never tell another living soul," Ellie promised. "Your privacy is safe with me, Mac. I keep all my clients' business confidential—just as a doctor or lawyer would."

He smiled slightly through the haze of pain he was experiencing. "That's funny."

"What's funny?" she asked.

"I had a dream about Johanna. That's why I woke up at 0600."

"What was the dream about? Can you tell me?"

"I dreamed I went to her and told her she could live her life in peace, that I forgave her and myself for the way I'd screwed up the marriage. I wished her well, and I meant it."

"How beautiful. Sometimes, when people get pieces back, they have dreams the night they're brought

back, or a week or so later. That kind of confirms that
I did my job."

"What did I have of Johanna?"

"I was taken to the real world again for you, and I
saw Johanna in this beautiful, Victorian-decorated
room."

"That was our bedroom," he said. "She decorated
it herself."

"It was beautiful...." Ellie sighed. "I saw Johanna take off her wedding ring and a fairly large di-
amond solitaire, and put them in a jewelry box. When
I came in and told Johanna who I was and why I was
there, I asked her if she had anything that belonged to
you. She gave me a very sad smile, opened the jewelry
box and handed me the set of rings. She said they had
always belonged to you. I brought the rings back and
blew them into your heart and the top of your head."

"I'll be damned." Mac sat there in stunned silence.
He wiped his mouth with his hand. "No one knew
this, but Johanna sent back the rings after the divorce
became final. Usually, the woman keeps them, but she
didn't want any part of me, not even the rings."

Ellie hurt for Mac. "At least now you are both free
of each other. The feeling you had when you woke up
will continue, Mac."

"This happiness?"

"Yes."

"I thought that was just because of you."

She laughed shyly. "Don't be surprised if you hear
from Johanna very soon. Often when a person gets a
missing piece back, she'll get the urge to contact the

other party, without realizing why. Subconsciously, she knows something is different."

"This is fascinating," Mac said. "And I can't thank you enough for doing it—for both of us."

"You mean you believe me?"

"How could I not? You gave me two pieces of information no one else in the world knew."

"You sound a little amazed."

"I'm amazed at you, at your talent."

She smiled a little. "Now you see why I do it, Mac. Recovering soul pieces is a miracle. It's real, and it works. But I never try to make someone believe me. I let my work speak for me. In your case, you'll continue to get validation. If Johanna calls, let me know."

Mac shook his head. "If she calls, that will be a miracle in itself."

"Why?"

"Because when she moved out of Phoenix a year ago and went back East, she refused to give me her forwarding address. I guess she thought I was going to pursue her or something."

"Were you going to?"

"No. The day she slapped me in the kitchen, I knew it was over. Really over. We went to divorce court and I didn't fight it or her."

"I'm sure you've had a lot of time since to think about what you did wrong or could have done better?"

"Years." He laughed, suddenly lighter and happier than he could ever recall. He glanced up and saw his master sergeant, Gus Calhoon, heading for his door. "Listen, I've got to go, but I want to thank you. Can I pay you for this journey?"

"Of course not."

"Are you sure?"

"Remember, I work for small donations only. In your case, I'm treating you as I would a friend. I would never accept anything, Mac. It's just my way of helping out, that's all."

Frowning, Mac said, "You deserve something."

"Just say thank you," she told him with a laugh.

"Thank you, and you haven't heard the last of this—or me."

And as Mac turned his attention to the papers Gus presented for his signature, he couldn't decide which was more amazing—the story Ellie had just related, or the fact that he could accept her story as the absolute truth.

CHAPTER SEVEN

Mac jerked awake to the sound of the phone ringing next to his bed. Blearily, he looked at the digital clock. It was 5:30. Who would be calling at this time of morning? He rolled over, taking most of the covers with him as he reached for the phone. Through his haze, he prayed there were no more problems at Hangar 13.

"Major Stanford," he mumbled, easing into a sitting position.

"Sorry to call you so early, Mac, but I wanted to catch you before you went to work."

Mac's eyes widened; his hand tightened around the phone. "Johanna?"

Her laughter was light and soft. "I see you haven't forgotten me."

Rubbing his eyes quickly with his hand, he forced himself fully awake. "I never will. What's wrong? Are you okay?"

Again, Johanna laughed. "I'm fine. Better than fine, actually. I'm getting married. Anyway, I decided enough time had elapsed since we'd spoken—I wanted to see how you were doing, plus share my good news with you."

"I'm fine, fine." He blinked, trying to absorb it all. "And congratulations on the marriage." His heart gave a twinge, but he really did wish her the best.

"Bill is a stockbroker, Mac. He's got two young children. His wife, Sally, died of breast cancer two years ago. We met at a Greenpeace meeting about six months ago and—" she sighed "—things just sort of fell into place. For some reason, you popped into my mind recently, and I decided that I wanted to share the news with you. I hope you don't mind. I know we haven't been in touch since I left Phoenix, but I thought it was time to let bygones be bygones."

His heart beat a little harder and he smiled slightly. "I'm glad you called, and I'm glad you've found the right man." Johanna had always wanted a man who had a nice, steady job—the kind of job Mac would never have.

"He's very nice, Mac. Like you in some ways—driven."

"But he's a nine-to-fiver."

With a laugh, Johanna said, "Yes. Plus, he has two beautiful daughters, age four and six. They're wonderful, Mac. I'm just so happy. You know how badly I've always wanted children."

"I know," he whispered, his voice choking. Johanna had been unable to conceive, and it had been a great sorrow to both of them. "I'm happy for you, Johanna. I really am." Mac felt tears sting the backs of his eyes, but he didn't care. Johanna was a good woman; he'd loved her with all he had to give, but it just hadn't been enough. He hoped her second marriage would be a strong one.

"I didn't call to gloat, Mac. I just wanted to let you know I was doing okay."

"Thanks. I appreciate it."

"I'm sorry I left the way I did. Looking back on it, I realize I could have been more understanding... kinder."

"Look," he rasped, "neither of us was very good toward the end, especially me."

"I know...." Johanna brightened. "Tell me there's a special woman in your life?"

He smiled a little and looked out the window toward the East. The sun had yet to rise; the sky was a gentle, pale pink color. That was how he felt right now—fragile, and a little emotional. "There is a lady...."

"Wonderful! What's she like, Mac?"

"A lot different from you in some ways," he said with a smile, "but in other ways, a bit the same. She likes gardening."

"Does she mind the hours you spend with your first wife, the air force?"

Johanna had always accused him of considering her his second wife—that the air force got the majority of his attention whether he was on or off base. "No, I don't think she sees my job in the same light you did."

"I'm glad, Mac. Really glad—for both of you."

"Thanks."

"Listen, I have to run. I have a nine o'clock appointment and I don't want to be late. Can I keep in touch?"

"Sure."

"I'll send you my new address and phone number."

Mac smiled. "I'm glad things are working out for you, Johanna. You deserve the happiness."

"And so do you, Mac. I loved you. You know that."

"Yes." His throat tightened.

"I hope your life is as happy as mine is. I'll stay in touch a little more often, okay?"

"Okay, Tiger." That had been the pet name he'd given her when they'd first met.

Johanna laughed softly. "Take good care of yourself, Major Stanford."

"I will. Goodbye...."

Mac sat there on the edge of the bed, his hands clasped between his thighs. He heard the birds singing gaily outside the bedroom window he'd left open to allow in the cool desert breeze. With a shake of his head, he smiled. It had been less than two days since Ellie's journey, and, true to her prediction, Johanna had called...right on schedule. Coincidence? Perhaps. But Mac didn't really think so....

He made his way into the bathroom, his heart filled with a lot of old emotions and his head with memories. As he glanced at himself in the mirror, rubbing the growth of beard on his face, he saw his eyes. For some reason, they looked clearer—somehow cleaner. How could that be? Did his soul recovery that Ellie performed change a person not only emotionally, but physically? He made a mental note to ask her.

As he took a hot, almost scalding shower—part of his normal morning routine—he was deluged by memories of his marriage to Johanna. The old hurts just kept bubbling up as he scrubbed and washed his hair, and just as miraculously they seemed to lift and then dissolve. It was an odd sensation, something he'd never experienced before.

Hurrying through his shaving and grabbing a flight suit, Mac decided to detour to Ellie's home before heading for Luke. He had to share this wonderful event with her, despite the early hour. He hurried through a quick breakfast of toast and strawberry jam, grabbed his briefcase and cap and was out the door.

Ellie was sitting on a bench in the middle of her garden, a cup of coffee in hand, when she heard a car pull up in front of the house. It was only six-thirty in the morning. Who could it be? She heard the car door open and shut. Before she could get to her feet, Mac appeared at the side of the house.

"Mac!"

He grinned and held up his hand. "I know this is impromptu. Got a few minutes?" Ellie was dressed in jeans and a fuchsia-colored T-shirt; she was barefoot, as she'd been the first time they'd met. Her hair was loose and spilling across her shoulders, long and beautiful—like her. He'd never been so happy to see anyone in his life. She looked so right here in her garden, as if she was a natural part of the colorful flowers and plentiful vegetables that surrounded her.

Ellie saw the gleam in Mac's eyes. He was freshly showered and shaved. His walk was almost a bounce, with his shoulders thrown proudly back, and a devilish grin hovered around that wonderfully shaped mouth of his. It made him look even more handsome than usual.

"You look ecstatic," she observed as he reached her.

"I am. Actually," Mac said as he sat down next to her on the redwood bench, "I wanted to share the fact that my ex-wife, Johanna, called me out of the blue this morning. You were right, Ellie."

She smiled and held her cup in her lap. "That's wonderful. It must have been a very good phone call— you're so happy."

"I'm beginning to appreciate your ability to observe."

Flushing, Ellie avoided his direct, hungry stare. "I think the more a person moves into his right brain, his intuitive, knowing side, the more he will sense about another. You're smiling, so it's pretty safe to assume you're happy."

He chuckled. "If nothing else, Ellie, you're humble about your talents." He proceeded to tell her about Johanna's call.

Ellie knew from the journey she'd taken the other day that there had still been a lot of unresolved feelings between Mac and his ex-wife. But she didn't mind hearing about it. She was content to sit there with him, absorbing the pleasure of having him near for a few, precious moments.

By the time Mac had finished with the story, she was smiling broadly. "It has all worked out for both of you," she murmured, placing her empty coffee cup down on the bricks next to the bench. She gently brushed his cheek with her fingers. It was a completely spontaneous gesture, and she was startled by her own action. So was Mac, but she saw the predatory, hunterlike intensity reappear in his eyes—that undeniable hunger for her.

"Your eyes even look clearer," she observed.

Mac sat very still after Ellie's work-worn fingers had grazed the flesh of his cheek. How long had he hoped she'd reach out and touch him? It was a simple, momentary gesture, but it spoke volumes. He saw high color come to her dusky cheeks, and saw the regret in her eyes. The smile he gave her was very male and very gentle.

"I noticed that myself this morning when I looked in the bathroom mirror. Does it have something to do with this soul recovery?"

Breathing a sigh of relief that Mac wasn't going to pursue her spontaneous gesture toward him, Ellie said, "The eyes always clear first. I've had cases where clients have been cured of chronic conditions. The soul is a powerful thing, Mac." She gave him a significant look.

"Makes sense to me," he said. He shook his head. "This is all so incredible. I feel so good today."

"Well," Ellie whispered, "I think getting to talk to Johanna helped you a lot. It isn't just the soul recovery. You had a lot of unfinished business with her after the divorce."

Rubbing his chin, Mac nodded. "Now it's complete."

"Life is always interesting to me," Ellie murmured. "When one cycle closes, another always opens up, presenting us with new opportunities, new leases on life." She met his sparkling hazel gaze, which spoke of the joy he was feeling inwardly. "Not that it means everything is going to be good, it just means we're ready to handle another level of experience."

"I like your philosophy," Mac said. He rose and smiled. "I've got to go. I don't want to, but I've got a busy day ahead of me."

Ellie stood and walked at his side. The day was turning warm already, common for a desert clime in the summer. She wanted to reach out and slip her hand into his, but knew she couldn't. Mac was so touchable, the kind of man who constantly invited her to reach out and touch him in some small, meaningful way. He didn't seem to react too much to the fact she'd touched his cheek earlier, and in a way, Ellie was grateful. What would she have done if he'd taken that touch as a signal to touch her back? Perhaps more intimately? A kiss? Heat went through her at that thought. She halted near the garage door.

He smiled down at her. "I don't know how I can thank you, Ellie."

"Don't try. I'm just glad you and your ex-wife are on friendly terms now."

Without thinking, Mac reached out and gently touched the crown of her head. Her hair was soft, thick and surprisingly sleek to his touch. "Thanks...."

Shaken, Ellie stood frozen beneath Mac's touch. Her scalp tingled wildly where he'd barely grazed her hair. She saw the naked hunger in his eyes, felt it swirl powerfully around her, like an invisible, molten embrace. Her mouth dry, she nodded, unable to speak.

As he walked back to his car, she stood there, cup in hand, her heart pounding erratically. It was some time before she recovered.

Mac knew there was trouble when he got out of his car and Gus Calhoon met him at the hangar door. But he was in too good a mood today to let anything get him down.

"Gus?"

"Major."

Mac headed to his office, the master sergeant on his heels. Once inside, Mac motioned for Gus to shut the door. The officer had a very unhappy look on his face.

"What's up, Gus?"

"Somethin' strange, Major."

"Oh?" Mac started prepping the coffeemaker.

"Yes, sir." Gus scratched his graying head. "At first I thought it was just a coincidence, but now I'm not so sure."

Mac twisted to look in his direction. "What are you talking about?"

"This is gonna sound crazy, sir, but a number of my people over the last couple of days have been getting bad headaches."

Frowning, Mac moved to his desk and sat down. "Headaches?"

"Yes, sir. Now, I didn't want to hit the panic button on this, but I had to send two of the crew home yesterday, and that's unusual. The funny thing is, once they left the hangar, their headaches went away. Now, how do you figure that one?"

Mac shrugged. "Could it be chemicals? Is everyone following regs on them?" A number of hazardous materials were used on base, but people were, for the most part, quite careful about handling them.

"My people follow the regs, Major. There are no open lids on any kind of haz-mat chemicals in the hangar."

Sitting back in his chair, Mac looked out across the large, cavernous hangar. Today, both ends of the structure were open, allowing the most air possible to circulate. On windy days, when sand was in the air, the doors were slid shut and the place became more stuffy. "Are the people who are getting the headaches prone to that kind of thing?"

"No.... Funny thing, though—most of them are women."

"Headaches can be a sign of unhappiness, Gus. Is there a situation out there I'm not aware of? Some discontent brewing?" Mac prided himself on keeping close tabs on his crews, but between the IG and the strange goings-on in the hangar, it was possible he had missed something.

"No," Gus muttered, "we've got a pretty happy crew out there, Major. I don't know. I just don't know."

"I want you to double-check all haz-mat materials. Let's eradicate the physical possibilities. Give me a list of the names of all the people who have reported headaches. I don't know what else to do."

"I don't know either, sir. I'll get you that list."

Mac tapped his fingers against his desk after the master sergeant left. Glancing at his watch, he saw that

it was nearly 0830, and he had to fly at 0900. His intuition told him to call Ellie about the headaches.

Following that hunch, he dialed her number.

"Hello?"

"Ellie, it's Mac."

"Didn't I just see you an hour ago?" She laughed.

"Yeah, I'm like a bad habit," he teased. Then, he
frowned. "I need to discuss something with you."

Mac told her about the mysterious headaches suddenly cropping up in the hangar. "My gut told me to
call you, but I don't know what you can tell me about
this, if anything. It would be one thing if I had a
sloppy crew and chemicals were left around open or
not stored properly, but that's not the case. What do
you feel about this?"

"I think we've got more problems with that spirit,
Mac."

A few days ago, he would have laughed. Instead, he
sobered considerably. "Okay...explain what you're
saying."

"When I asked him to promise not to hurt your
people, I didn't think he'd do it, Mac. An angry spirit
with enough energy can literally attack people. Now,
you said that most of the people getting headaches
were women. I've found that women are just natu-
rally more in tune with their psychic side—they've got
their antennas up, if you will, more than men do. If
this spirit in the corner of the hangar isn't letting his
anger out by throwing objects, he could be attacking
the people working closest to the corner. I know it
sounds silly, but malevolent spirits can do a lot of

things that most people would never connect them with.''

"What's it doing? How can it give a person a headache?''

"A spirit that wants to stay earthbound has to suck energy off living beings every day, Mac. The more energy it gathers, the more powerful it becomes. Chances are, that spirit is sucking a lot of energy out of the auras of everyone who works in that hangar.

"A person would feel literally drained, lose her energy and feel very tired afterward. In this case, I'll bet the spirit is draining the energy out of these women, and that's why they're getting headaches.''

Rubbing his chin, Mac nodded, and through the windows, watched his people working around the two jets in the hangar. "How could I prove this, Ellie?''

"Check to see if the people who are getting the headaches work nearest to that corner. Some spirits get territorial, and don't like to range too far from their source. In this case, the spirit is going to attack those nearest to him.''

"Okay.'' He sighed. "I'll tell you, this sounds bizarre.''

Ellie said, "I know. You're just not used to dealing with the invisible part of our lives, that's all. Do me a favor, will you? After you check out the situation, give me a call back and let me know?''

"Sure,'' Mac said. "Right now, I've got to slug down a cup of hot coffee and then fly. I'll have my master sergeant find out the information. When I get back off the flight, I'll give you a call.''

"Fine.''

"Ellie?"

"Yes?"

"I want you to know I think you're a very special person."

"You're kind of special yourself, Major Stanford."

He smiled slightly. "Special enough for you to say yes to me taking you out to dinner tonight?"

Ellie hesitated. "Yes, I'd like that."

Relief flooded through Mac, and he grinned broadly. His boldness had paid off. "Good. I'll give you a call later."

Ellie was eating her lunch when the phone rang. The voice on the other end of the line was instantly recognizable.

"How was your flight, Mac?"

"Great, as always. Only one thing wrong."

"What was that?"

"My lady was missing from the rear seat."

Closing her eyes, she smiled to herself. "You're more of a romantic than I gave you credit for, Major."

His laugh was husky. "I don't know. I found myself thinking about our dinner engagement the whole time I was romping around in the sky. Maybe there's hope for me, after all."

She relaxed against the doorjamb, the phone cradled between her cheek and shoulder. "What do you mean?"

"Johanna always hated the time that my flying took away from our relationship. Back then, I was doing a lot more of it, because I was training young pilots. Now I'm not."

"I don't begrudge your flight time, Mac. You need to fly. Eagles are never happy when they're shackled to Mother Earth."

"Thanks for understanding."

"So, what did you find out about the headaches?"

"Gus took a check, and you're right—the people working closest to that corner of the hangar are the ones getting the headaches. One crew consists of all women, and they're the ones getting them."

She sighed. "Looks like I'm going to have to come back to the hangar and try to get rid of that spirit once and for all. At least it isn't throwing tools around, so that's an improvement of sorts."

"Let's talk about that over dinner tonight."

"Okay. Do you have a place in mind?"

"I have a favorite seafood restaurant that flies fresh catch in from San Diego every day. Are you a fish lady?"

"I love fish."

"Okay, it's a date. Wear something fancy, because this is a pretty formal place for the Southwest."

Ellie groaned. "Mac, I don't wear heels. I wouldn't be caught dead in them."

Laughing, Mac said, "Sweetheart, no matter what you wear, I'm sure it will be fine. You're usually barefoot when I see you—I knew you weren't going to put those torturous things on your feet."

"You understand!"

He chuckled. "My women crew members in-

formed me a long time ago about the dangers of heels.
They wear boots and like it.''

"I'm not into boots, but I'll try to come up with
something acceptable.''

"Good. I'll meet you at 1800. I mean six p.m.''

Her heart beat a little more strongly, and Ellie
gripped the phone. Mac had called her sweetheart, an
endearment. How could she get him to understand
that there was no future for them? Her past was still
too much in her present. Yet she couldn't bring herself to tell him that. He was such a vital man, a man
who loved life, grabbed it and lived it every moment.
Ellie hadn't met many people with that kind of en-
thusiasm, that kind of bravery. And she couldn't bear
to burst his bubble.

"I'll see you at 1800, Mac...."

She set the phone on the hook and wrapped her
arms around herself. Her sister, Diana, would laugh
at her for even thinking of getting involved with a man
in the military. With a shake of her head, Ellie went
back to the table to finish her sandwich. But every
time she pictured Mac's strong, handsome features in
her mind's eye, her pulse accelerated. What did her
body know that her head didn't?

CHAPTER EIGHT

Ellie nervously wiped her damp hands down her pale pink cotton skirt as she saw Mac pull up in front of her house. It was exactly six p.m. He emerged from the car dressed in a charcoal gray suit, white shirt and dark blue tie. He looked like some very successful executive who owned his own business. Her heart speeded up as he walked confidently to her front door and rang the doorbell. All day she'd asked herself what she had agreed to when she'd said she'd go to dinner with Mac. Was it a commitment? What kind of commitment?

Nervously touching the long, free strands of hair near the side of her face, Ellie answered the door. She was worried she didn't look dressed up enough, but she couldn't be someone she wasn't.

"You look beautiful," Mac murmured in greeting as Ellie opened the door. The tea-length pink skirt emphasized her curvaceous figure, and the white leather sandals matched the color of the very feminine, short-sleeved blouse with venetian lace at the throat. She wore long, beaded earrings that emphasized the Indian qualities of her face, and her hair was loose just the way he liked it. Mac scolded himself silently as he saw Ellie blush hotly at his intense inspection. He had to learn to control himself.

"Thank you," she whispered, stepping aside. "Let me get my shawl, and I'll be right with you." She hurried down the hall to her bedroom, feeling shaky, needy and wonderful all at once. Mac's eyes had burned with desire. Desire for her. She picked up a pale pink crocheted shawl and draped it over her left arm, along with her white leather purse.

Mac smiled and held out his hand to Ellie as she reappeared. "I hope you're hungry."

She was hungry, all right, but her yearning was all for Mac. How wonderfully handsome he looked! She was afraid to tell him that, afraid that he might get the wrong idea, and perhaps overstep the unspoken boundaries that still existed between them.

"It has been a busy day, so I'm ready to eat," Ellie assured him as he guided her out the door. She turned and made sure it was locked. The evening sky over Phoenix was a pale yellow, and it was still blisteringly hot.

Once they were in the car and headed for The Cove, a very exclusive, five-star restaurant, Mac wanted to share some news with Ellie. "The provost marshal's office contacted me late this afternoon about the guy who was AWOL."

They were driving down I 17, the main freeway through this sprawling part of Phoenix. Ellie watched as palm trees and colorful oleanders in pink, white and red flashed by. "Oh?"

"The office had sent out an APB to all surrounding law-enforcement officials at the time of his disappearance. I talked to Captain Rupert today, and she said that not only was a local and regional APB put out on him, but his name was logged into the FBI files, too.''

''Is that normal procedure, I wonder?''

''I don't know.'' Mac glanced over at her, unable to get enough of her thoughtful, serene features, her very serious dark brown eyes. ''The FBI did some checking in his state and hometown and never found any proof of his return. If he was AWOL at all.''

''What do you think now, knowing this, Mac?''

''It looks to me like murder is a much stronger possibility. Usually, AWOL people show up sooner or later at their folks' home, or at a sibling's. That's why we're usually able to find these people and bring them to justice within the military system.''

''I know this man is dead. I just don't know if it was murder or not.''

Frowning, Mac turned off the freeway and onto the Bethany Home Road exit. The setting sun was glaring and he was glad he wore his aviator's sunglasses. ''I don't want to mix business with pleasure, Ellie, but I think we need to take the next step in doing something about this spirit at Hangar 13. What do you think?'' He braked at the stoplight, then turned right when traffic on the busy street had cleared.

''I agree with you. The fact that he's attacking the crews closest to his corner is a sign that he's discontent. He'll probably continue to move outward from the original territory that he established as his in the corner of that hangar.''

''I worry about you,'' Mac confided. He slowed and made a left turn into a large asphalt parking lot. The Cove was in an austere-looking building, fairly nondescript and easily missed. Mac had often found that the best things in life were tastefully understated—like Ellie.

"I'll be okay," she reassured him.

"How do you know?" He parked the car, then looked at her profile, the way her full lips were pursed.

"Because my chief guide has never placed me in a situation beyond my capabilities. If she didn't feel I could handle it properly, she would tell me not to become involved in the first place."

He sighed and opened the door. "It makes sense, but I'm jumpy because I don't know anything about the other worlds you work in. And what I don't know or understand worries me, especially when it involves *you*."

To Ellie's surprise, there was a dance floor at the rear of the exclusive, very expensive restaurant. A five-piece ensemble played ballroom music from the thirties and forties. After a delicious dinner of fresh sea bass, Ellie was ready to get up and move. Mac grinned, pulled out her chair for her and escorted her to the other room, where several other couples were already dancing. First they would enjoy their after-dinner coffee. And then dancing would be the order of the night.

"I like this place because you can eat all you want and work it off all in the same night," Mac teased as they took a table in the corner of the room, away from the music, so they could talk in a fairly normal tone of voice.

A waitress came over and Mac ordered coffee. He turned to Ellie when the waitress was gone and folded his hands on the ivory linen tablecloth. "Now that a very enjoyable dinner is over, do you feel up to discussing some business?"

"Sure." Ellie was very relaxed in Mac's presence. How could she have been so nervous before?

Mac looked around at the semidarkened room and then devoted his full attention to her. In the shadows, Ellie's large, prominent eyes were expressive and luminous. He wondered what they would look like after he kissed her. The thought had been hanging over him all night, nudging him, coercing him, refusing to leave his mind. The shadows were loving to Ellie's Cherokee features, her high cheekbones and clean jawline. But no matter what light she was placed in, she always looked beautiful.

Clearing his throat, he said, "I can scrub a night repair on two jets tomorrow evening and you could come over and get rid of this spirit in the hangar if you want."

She smiled a little, resting her chin on her folded hands. The gleam in Mac's eyes, that intense, hooded look that always sent her heart racing, was there again. Because she was so open to other's vibrations, she could feel Mac's desire for her. Did he realize he was actually touching her with his thoughts, with his needs? Ellie was sure he wasn't. If he was, he'd be mortified. She didn't want that. Mac had been the epitome of a gentleman all evening and hadn't once reached out and touched her. Not that that would be so bad....

"That will be fine. My last appointment for tomorrow is at noon."

"Good. What time would you like to do this?"

The waitress brought over their coffee, and Ellie waited until she'd left before answering. "Three a.m. is best, Mac."

"Why 0300?"

"That's high tide in the universe, in an energy sense." She took a sip of the fragrant Columbian coffee from the delicate white china cup rimmed with gold. Setting the cup on the saucer, she said, "Our twenty-four-hour day has invisible shifts of energy linked to it." With a gesture toward the ceiling, she added, "Energy ebbs and flows to and from us just like our great oceans come in and go out on a daily basis. My mother taught us that three in the afternoon is 'low tide' in a universal energy sense, and that 'high tide' is at three in the morning. This ebb and flow is like the cosmos breathing, Mac. Have you ever heard of the postprandial dip? Science has determined that cells multiply at their slowest rate at three in the afternoon, and at their fastest at three in the morning."

"Fascinating," Mac said.

Spending time with Ellie was like flying—something that was absolutely necessary to Mac's soul, his spirit...and his heart. He knew she was gun-shy, that he should try to be patient, but he was not a patient man. "Maybe I'm out of line for saying this," Mac told her huskily, "but being around you is like flying to me."

Ellie's pulse bounded once, with joy. She saw the burning hunger in Mac's eyes, and allowed the caress of his deep voice to touch her in all ways. "What a beautiful compliment," she whispered.

He reached out and captured one of her hands. "Come on, let's dance."

Without hesitation, Ellie stood up. She'd been looking forward to this moment, hoping that Mac was a dancer. The music was soft and slow, and so much of her ached to be in Mac's arms, to be against that tall, stalwart frame.

There were a number of other couples on the dance floor, but there was plenty of room. Ellie smiled up into Mac's dark, shadowed face as he took her into his arms. He allowed her to dictate the distance between them. There was such a naturalness to it that she found herself barely touching him here and there, at the point of their hips, his chest lightly pressed against her breasts. Her entire body tingled wildly as his arm slid around her waist and he captured her. It was a wonderful feeling, a giddy one for Ellie. How long had it been since she'd allowed a man to hold her this way? *Far too long,* her heart whispered. She ignored the warnings her head was sending her.

Whether it was the music or just Mac's presence, Ellie found herself resting her cheek against his shoulder. His large hand fit perfectly in the small of her back, drawing her a little closer to him. They moved as if they were breathing together, their hearts in unison with one another. Ellie marveled at his grace as they danced; he led without jerking her around, led in a way that made every cell in her body yearn for more contact with him. She was aware of the pounding drum of his heart; she could feel it through her body. Although Mac was tall and lean, and she, shorter and more rounded, they seem to fit perfectly together—like some long-lost puzzle pieces that had finally found one another.

She surrendered to Mac's arms, to his guidance, as they glided across the wooden dance floor. Ellie heard the music, but more important, she was heatedly aware of Mac's touch against her back, of his hand capturing hers. She felt him quiver almost imperceptibly as she laid her cheek on the lapel of his suit. Smiling, she closed her eyes, never more in sync with a man, never happier.

"You're like some wonderful dream," Mac whispered in her ear, his hand tightening against her as they danced. "When I was a teenager, I used to imagine what it would be like to meet the woman of my dreams." He eased back enough to look down into her half-closed eyes, which were luminous with wisdom and emotion. His mouth curved ruefully. "You are that woman to me. You know that, don't you?"

Ellie barely nodded. She parted her lips to say something, but the overwhelming desire threading through her made her lose track of her thoughts. She gazed up at Mac's dark, shadowy eyes, wildly aware that he wanted to kiss her. Should she let him? What would it mean if she did? What would change between them? Was she capable of dealing with it? The questions made her hesitate, and she saw a newfound tenderness in Mac's eyes, as if he'd just heard her questioning herself, as if he were mentally and emotionally in tune with her predicament.

Mac saw the fear, the question and the desire burning in Ellie's eyes. Did she realize just how beautiful she was to him? He didn't think so. He acquiesced to her needs, not his. She would have to make the first move to kiss him; he wouldn't rush her. This was too important to Mac to botch it by behaving like some out-of-control teenager with raging hormones.

As he danced with Ellie in his arms, he decided that dreams really did come true, and he wished he could have shared that thought with her—but now wasn't the time. She was like hot, fluid sunlight in his arms, her movements so graceful and synchronized with his that she appeared to anticipate his every move. As the music ended, he opened his arms to allow her to step back from him. There was such tenderness burning in her eyes as she lifted those thick, black lashes to stare up at him in wonderment. He stroked her hair tenderly.

"Come on," he murmured, "it's almost midnight and I've got to get you home, whether I want to or not."

"I wish," she said as he walked her slowly to the parking lot, his arm around her waist, "that we were out on the desert, hiking. I wish we could look up and see those beautiful stars in the sky."

Mac opened the car door for her. As she left the curve of his arm, he met and caught her luminous gaze. "We can make that happen, you know."

Hesitating, Ellie nodded. "I know...."

Mac saw the sorrow in her eyes, the hope dying in them. As she slipped into the car and he shut the door, he wondered if her sadness was over the fact she could never become that close, that intimate with him because he was a foreigner, an alien to her world, her beliefs. *One day at a time,* Mac warned himself. Look how Ellie was beginning to trust him. Hadn't there been progress? Yes, definite progress. So why should he feel so panicky? Feel as if the sunbeam he'd captured eagerly, selfishly, in his hands would escape and never really be his?

Ellie hesitated at the porch of her home. Mac had a serious look on his face now, and she wondered if her decision not to kiss him on the dance floor had something to do with it. She felt a little guilty, but realized she must be true to herself first.

"It was a beautiful evening, Mac. Thank you." She reached out and touched his cheek, the prickling sensation of his recently shaved beard racing up her fingertips.

Mac caught Ellie's hand and squeezed it. He saw desire leap to her eyes, felt that tension tighten between them, but he hesitated. He could almost taste Ellie's lips beneath his—he wanted to kiss her that badly. A momentary hesitation on her part as he pulled her forward warned him off. Swallowing his disappointment, he said, "How about if I meet you at the guard gate at 0230?"

Her senses spinning, her heart pounding, Ellie felt her mouth going dry. How she wanted to kiss Mac! Nothing had ever seemed so right, but the fear in her head kept her from moving forward into his arms. "Y-yes, that would be fine," she heard herself say, her voice sounding oddly hollow and distant. Mac gave her a reassuring smile as he strode off, as if to say he understood. Ellie prayed he really did.

At 2:30, Mac met Ellie at the front gate of Luke Air Force Base. The base was nearly deserted at this time of morning, and they drove over to Hangar 13 without incident. The desert air was dry and a bit chilly as they walked into the hangar area.

"I had the planes taken out this evening before my crew left," he told her. Mac had had both ends of the hangar shut with the entire area sealed off, so no one would hear the beat of the drum and come around to investigate.

Ellie nodded. The hair on the back of her neck was standing up, and she felt a cold chill work its way down her spine. Most of the lights were off, so the interior of the hangar looked gloomy and forbidding. She knelt on the concrete floor and opened her drum case.

"Here, you're going to need this," she told him.

Mac took the drum and the stick. He gestured to two chairs he'd placed in the opposite corner from where the entity lived. "Over here." He felt a bit tense. He saw the worry in Ellie's eyes, too.

"Are you okay?" he asked.

"Yes, fine. . . ."

"You don't look it."

Ellie halted at the chairs and allowed her gaze to move to the entity's corner. "Since the last time I was here, I feel a higher level of malevolence," she said.

"What does that mean?" Mac sat down, the round drum resting on his thighs.

Ellie wiped her hands against her slacks. She wore loose, cotton clothing and a pair of sneakers. "I can feel his hatred, his anger. It's as if he's twice as powerful as the last time I came here." She shook her head. "Sometimes," she murmured as she sat down next to Mac, "when a spirit knows that it's going to be asked to move on, it gets very agitated and begins to suck energy from anyone and everyone it can." Gesturing toward that corner, she added, "The spirit doesn't want to leave, so it begins to stockpile energy to fight off the person who's going to ask it to go."

"Sort of like stocking up ammunition?" Mac guessed.

Grimly, Ellie nodded. "Exactly."

"Well, is it dangerous?"

"It can be." She sat quietly for a moment, absorbing the vibes in the room. "I can feel his agitation, and he's very combative, Mac."

Scowling, he muttered, "Then maybe you shouldn't do it, Ellie. I don't want you hurt."

She felt his concern, and tried to smile. "I *want* to do it. I'll know a lot more when I move into my altered state, Mac." She reached out and touched his arm. "The worst that can happen is that it will attack me."

"And if it does, what then?" Mac didn't like this conversation. He didn't like the possibility that Ellie could be hurt. Worst of all, there was absolutely nothing he could do to protect her if something happened. That bothered him more than anything else.

Ellie shrugged. "I've been attacked before, Mac. Usually I become drained of my auric energy. If that happens, I become very weak and usually can't walk a straight line. It can affect me physically for upwards of twenty-four hours. If it should occur again, I'll have to sleep it off. My natural ability to restore the energy to my own aura will take place within a day of the attack."

"Can these things really injure you, though?"

Ellie saw the worry in Mac's eyes. "In a worst-case scenario, it could—conceivably—kill me, but that's not going to happen. I'll be okay."

Shocked at her statement, Mac tightened his grip on the drum. He was wildly aware of Ellie's warm hand on his arm. She was so alive, so vibrant with life, that he'd never entertained the thought that this kind of work could kill someone. "Are you serious?" he croaked.

"I am." Her fingers tightened on the hard length of his arm. "Mac, it's not going to happen. I think you should know and understand what is going on. Most discarnate spirits can't hurt a fly."

"But this one already has. It throws tools, for starters."

"Yes," she allowed, "I know." Releasing his arm, she turned to face the corner. Their voices floated eerily around the hangar, echoing and reechoing. "The worst that will happen if things get out of hand is I'll feel some weakness. That's all."

"And if it happens?"

"Then take me home and tuck me into my bed," she said gently. "Just let me sleep it off, and I'll be okay." When she read the disbelief in his eyes, she said, "Trust me on this, Mac. Okay?"

Frowning, he nodded. "This way I feel about you, Ellie, I don't want you in any kind of danger—whether I think it can happen or not."

"I know," she said sympathetically. Mac was having a problem in believing any of this could happen. Still, he believed her enough to be genuinely worried, and he was obviously torn. "You just keep a steady beat on that drum, no matter what happens. If I have to combat this spirit, it's vital that you keep me in that altered state, Mac. If I do get attacked, don't stop beating the drum."

"I'll stop when you tell me to stop."

"Exactly." She took a deep breath. "I'm ready."

He wasn't. There was such dread within Mac that he hesitated. Was he crazy? Did he actually feel the anger and hatred? Or was it his imagination? The unsettled feeling in the hangar was tightening around his neck like a noose. Was that how Ellie felt? Mac finally decided the best way he could help Ellie was by doing exactly as she asked.

"Okay. How long do you think this will take?"

"Probably no longer than half an hour—maybe forty-five minutes."

He nodded, his voice turning raspy. "Just be careful, Ellie. Please..."

Touched to the point of tears, Ellie whispered, "I will be, don't worry." She turned and settled into the straight-backed chair, closed her eyes and began to take deep, measured breaths.

Mac settled into his own chair, lifted the drum off his thighs and held it tightly in his left hand. His mouth a grim line, he began a solid, steady drumbeat. If only he could see, hear or feel what Ellie did, it would be so much easier on him! Was she in danger? An uncharacteristic chill worked up his spine, and he trembled. He might not be clairvoyant like Ellie, but in his gut, he felt something was dreadfully wrong. The beat of the drum sounded heavily, authoritatively, throughout the gloomy depths of the hangar. The sound echoed eerily through the cavernous building. His head seemed to pound in unison with the beat of the drum.

Mac glanced over at Ellie out of the corner of his eyes. He saw her clean, Native American profile, and felt some of his ridiculous fear dissolve. She looked so serene, her hands relaxed on her thighs, her arms at ease against her body. When he gazed at her, he saw only peace, not combat, not fear and certainly not death. But as he studied her more closely, he saw, to his surprise, small dots of perspiration beginning to appear on her upper lip. What was going on? What was she seeing in that altered state?

Dread washed through Mac, sharp and clean, like a knife twisting in his gut and then thrusting upward toward his heart. He sensed a change—an incredible, lightninglike change in the atmosphere that surrounded them. Suddenly he felt as if someone had hit him in the chest. His breath was knocked out of him, as if he had fallen hard to the ground. Blinking, Mac opened his mouth to suck in a breath of air. What the hell was going on? Quickly, he looked at Ellie. Horror washed over him. Her face, once dusky and vital, now looked pasty and washed-out. It was as if all the color had been sucked out of her, leaving her a thin, gray ghost of her former self. He saw sweat standing out all over her face. Her hands were clenched into fists resting tensely on her thighs.

What was going on? *What?* He wanted to scream. He felt the surge of hatred, anger and murderous intensity reach out and slam into him. His hand faltered, and the drumbeat began to fail. No! More than anything, he had to keep drumming, or something terrible, something permanent, could happen to Ellie. In that moment he knew, with a clarity that transcended all his fears, that he was falling in love with her. But the terrible intensity of the other feelings swirled, eddied and struck at him again. He felt as if he was losing his mind.

Mac had no chance to worry about Ellie; he was in his own battle for his sanity. The grayness of the hangar blurred before his eyes, and he felt as if he was being torn apart by invisible hands. He couldn't think; it was as if something had ripped his rational, logical mind out of his head. All he could do as he wrestled with the strange sensations and unexpected feelings was keep beating that drum. Ellie's life, and the life he wanted to share with her someday, hinged on his drumming.

The desire to breathe began to be taken from him. He couldn't believe it. Mac forced himself to think about breathing, about sucking huge, deep drafts of

air into his lungs. It made no sense. How could he
suddenly want to stop? Breathing was an automatic
function of the physical body. Nothing short of a heart
attack could make him want to stop. Again his beating on the drum faltered. Mac scrambled inwardly.
Focus! He had to focus. And then, suddenly, he remembered what Ellie had said: that focus, like a laser
of concentration, was the only thing that kept her safe.
It could keep him safe, too. Mac had needed that kind
of focus in the past, in his jet, when he was locked in
a deadly game up in the sky with an enemy plane. He
brought that same intense concentration to bear on
himself now.

Gasping for air, he forced himself to think about
breathing, about beating the drum, keeping up that
same, deep, sonorous beat. He was in such personal
peril that he couldn't even look over to see how Ellie
was doing. Mac felt as if he were in a battle for his life
with some unseen, yet violently dangerous opponent.
Sweat popped out on his forehead, trickled down his
ribs. His gasps were audible, labored. He couldn't
think; it was taking all his effort simply to keep
breathing.

What about Ellie? It took the last drop of his
strength to even think the thought. No! No, she
couldn't be hurt! She couldn't be wounded by this
thing, this invisible, murderous spirit. Mac no longer
doubted anything Ellie had ever shared with him.
Whatever was swirling around them like a vicious,
unleashed storm was real. His entire physical body was
responding to it. He knew this wasn't in his head. And
if he felt this way, how did Ellie feel? Was she receiv-

ing the brunt of this attack? *My God,* he thought, *she could die.* And all he could do was keep beating the drum. His hand was sweaty, and the drumstick kept slipping out of his grasp. But he kept on, knowing that his drumming was the only thing standing between Ellie and death.

Suddenly, the drum was like a cognizant, verbal heartbeat. It was about *life.* There was some subtle yet definite shift within Mac as he thought about the drum in these symbolic terms. Ellie had said that the drum echoed the heartbeat of Mother Earth. He didn't know what that meant, but he did understand on some primal level that the drum was Ellie's lifeline. He couldn't let her down. He wouldn't....

CHAPTER NINE

The last thing Ellie expected was that the entity would attack Mac. She had just gotten into her altered state with the steady beat of the drum when she saw a roiling, dark cloud of energy moving rapidly toward them. Instantly, her spirit guides stepped between her and the furious, attacking spirit. Her heart was pounding hard in her chest, and she was simultaneously aware of her physical being and of her altered, interdimensional state.

She saw the entity come speeding out of the dark, a moving cloud of negative energy, and slam full force into Mac's chest. To her horror, she realized that it was trying to kill Mac by striking him hard enough through his aura to stop the beating of his heart.

Ellie broke one of the most important rules of shamanic journeying. Instead of allowing her spirit guides to stop the attack against Mac, she moved between them. Her reaction was instinctive, unthinking. She was falling in love with Mac, and she had to protect the one she loved.

Because she had stepped in front of Mac's aura to protect him, Ellie had no protection in place for herself. Her spirit guides couldn't move fast enough to counter the shrieking, furious entity. The spirit howled like a banshee and turned his attack to her. A blow, hard and swift, reverberated through Ellie's being. She gasped, barely able to get her breath. Throwing up her hands, she cried out, "Stop! I mean you no harm!"

Valiantly, Ellie tried to gather her strewn emotions and focus her badly mauled energy. She felt drained and knew instantly that the entity had struck her in the solar-plexus chakra, located in the region of her stomach. Nausea rolled through her, and she tried to ignore the feeling as she watched the entity back off— just for a moment.

Seizing the opportunity, Ellie said, "I come in peace. I mean you no harm. Please, tell me your name and what I can do to help you."

"Bah! You lie woman! You come to make me go and I won't do it. You aren't powerful enough to stop me!"

Ellie saw the spirit's face contort until it looked like a caricature of a dragon, his lips pulled away from his teeth, his eyes small and red. Desperately, she tried to stop the leak of energy from her aura, realizing belatedly just how much strength she was losing. She felt weak, very weak, and her brain was faltering from the shocking loss of auric "blood." Her spirit guides were in place now, but if she didn't keep her focus, the entity could attack her again. She could feel sweat forming on her face and trickling down the sides of her rib cage; her heart was hammering as if she were about to enter cardiac arrest. Ellie knew her physical body was mirroring the attack that had occurred in her aura.

She wanted to find out how Mac was doing; she could hear the drumbeat faltering slightly, but she didn't dare shift her focus one iota, or the malevolent spirit would take advantage of her lapse of concentration and attack—and this time, she would not survive. Ellie understood that the entity was completely capable of killing her; she could see it in his tortured features.

As a shaman, Ellie had been taught a long time ago never to fear death; shamans in training frequently went through dismemberment in the inner dimensions to get rid of their fear of dying. She wasn't afraid of death, but she was afraid for Mac, because he had no training, no real protection from something like this. More than anything else, she had to keep the entity's attention and lure it away from Mac.

Ellie moved toward the corner where it made its home, knowing she was taking a tremendous risk. As she moved closer with her spirit guides like soldiers on the front line protecting her, she saw the being turn. A howl tore from his mouth and he lunged toward her.

"Get out! Get out!"

Ellie steeled herself for the attack. This time, her guardians took the major brunt of the spirit's blow. Still, her aura was shaken, and she trembled from the attempt. The entity bounced backward, flying off his feet. He scrambled upright and attacked again. With each lunge, Ellie felt herself weakening. She was so focused on the confrontation that she no longer physically heard the drum beating, although she was peripherally aware of the vibration. How badly she wanted to come out of the journeying state and make sure Mac was all right! But she didn't dare.

The entity made four attacks. After the last one, he stood there panting, his head hung, his fists clenched a few feet from Ellie's guardians. The dark clouds swirled like a hurricane around him, and to her surprise and terror, they began to grow larger and more threatening. She'd never realized how much power this entity had, and it was impossible to know such a thing until she confronted him.

"I mean you no harm," Ellie began gently. "I am here to help you, if I can."

The spirit looked up, glaring at her. "You can help by leaving! You have no right to be here. This is my home! You are a trespasser!"

Ellie raised one hand in a gesture of peace. "No, *you* trespass! You are dead, you have left your physical shell. You should move on, to the light world."

The entity snorted violently and shook his fist at her. "Stupid woman! I own this place! I don't have to go anywhere I don't want to go!"

"You are attacking other people," Ellie told him angrily, "and that is wrong."

The entity grinned and slowly relaxed. "It is my privilege to take what I want from whomever I want."

"No," Ellie rattled in a low, off-key voice, "you don't have such a right. What can I do to help you move into the light world?"

"Nothing!" He made a cutting gesture with his hand. "You have not caught my murderer! I wait for him to come back, so I may take his life." He clenched his fist and shook it at Ellie. "I go nowhere until he's caught! He took my life without my permission. A life for a life."

Ellie understood the spirit's desire to attack the man who had killed him. "Can you tell me his name?" She held her breath, hoping against hope that the arrogant being would cooperate.

"His name is William Treadwell."

"What else can you tell me about him?" Ellie was relieved the spirit was going to finally give them some information. She felt herself weakening rapidly from the powerful attacks, and her concentration was slipping. Somehow, she had to get out of this state and back into the third dimension. Could she? She wasn't sure.

"I was off duty and came to the line shack. He killed me because I was dealing drugs, and he hadn't paid me for what he'd bought. Cocaine is expensive, and he refused to pay. When I hit him, he struck me and I fell, hitting my head on the corner of the desk. I died."

Ellie nodded. She moved slowly out of the entity's territory. "I will do what I can to bring this man to justice for you—"

"That is not what I want!" The spirit became agitated and moved swiftly back to the unoccupied corner of the hangar. "I want *him!* I want to kill him slowly. He took my life. He had no right!"

Backing away, Ellie felt the last of her reserves begin to dissolve. She felt herself drifting, her concentration faltering. If she didn't get back, she would be caught forever in the in-between worlds.

Her spirit guides could not help her return; it was up to her to do it. Blackness began to permeate Ellie's vision, and she felt her physical body sag. She had to return! Honing in with the last of her strength, she listened to the drum. And finally, her fear of being trapped propelled her back into the third dimension.

Mac saw Ellie suddenly sag in the chair, her lips parted, her body going limp. He stopped drumming just in time to grab one of her arms before she pitched toward the concrete floor of the hangar. He immediately put the drum aside. She looked terribly pale.

"Ellie?" Mac's voice was shaky as he got up. His own legs felt rubbery, but he forced himself to pull her off the chair and lay her down on the floor. For a brief second he thought she was dead. Wrapping two fingers across her wrist, he felt a very shallow, slow pulse. Thank God. She was still alive—but for how long?

Mac didn't know. His mind was shorting out, and it was tough to think two coherent thoughts. He had to get Ellie to the base dispensary for help. Crouching down, he slipped one arm beneath her neck and the other beneath her knees. When he lifted her, he realized just how weak he was. What had happened? He felt as if someone had sucker-punched him.

Something had gone terribly wrong, Mac realized as he carried Ellie to his car. The warm desert night surrounded them, and he saw the brilliant stars above. Ellie's comment about the stars went through his mind and heart. She had to be all right. She just had to.

"Well?" Mac demanded of the doctor on duty, "How is she?" He was agitated and angry. They had whisked Ellie off to a sheet-draped cubicle and he'd had to remain out in the lobby, waiting.

Dr. Gwen Johnson said, "She's stable, Major Stanford. We'll have to run some tests to find out what's wrong."

"Is she conscious?" Mac automatically clenched his fists and tried to steel himself for the answer.

"No. Her blood pressure is alarmingly low, but she's breathing normally. You say she just slid off the chair she was sitting on?"

Mac nodded. He hadn't told the young, blond-haired doctor the whole truth, but he hadn't lied about that. "That's right, Doctor. Look, may I see her?"

Dr. Johnson shrugged. "She's unconscious, Major."

"But she'll know I'm there," he insisted, the reins he held on his temper shredding. It was now 0500, and his nerves were frayed. He was feeling a panic he'd never experienced in his life.

"I don't mind. Go ahead," Dr. Johnson said. "Right now we're taking blood samples. It could be an epileptic seizure, a stroke—"

"It's none of those things," Mac growled, and rushed past the nonplussed doctor. He hurried down the hall to the emergency room, where he found Ellie alone on a gurney, covered with a white sheet. Gripping her limp, cool fingers, Mac stood at her side. The pallor of her face hadn't changed.

His mouth had a bitter coating and he swallowed hard against tears. Reaching over, Mac nudged several strands of hair away from Ellie's smooth brow. How soft her skin felt. How many times had he wanted to touch her like this, with a tender caress meant to convey how strongly he felt about her? Did

Ellie realize he was falling in love with her? Would she ever know?

Nothing mattered to Mac in that instant except to see Ellie's lashes lift and reveal those beautiful golden brown eyes of hers that were always so full of vitality. He whispered, "Ellie, I'm here. It's Mac. You're going to be all right. Do you hear me, sweetheart? You're going to be fine...."

He had no idea if she would be okay or not, but he wanted to soothe her. Could she hear him? Probably not, but just in case, he wanted her to know he was on hand, and that he would help her as much as he could. Right now, he felt inept and helpless. Frustration ate at him. If only he knew enough about Ellie's world to help her!

Again he fought back the urge to cry. Tears stung the backs of his eyes and he shut them tightly. It wouldn't be appropriate to have a major in the air force bawling his eyes out. He wrestled with his raw emotions for over a minute, but the lump in his throat refused to go away. He leaned down and rested his lips against Ellie's brow.

How cold her skin felt. He moved his lips softly against her forehead, so much emotion behind his chaste kiss. Straightening, he took her hand into both of his, as if to will the heat of his body into hers. Mac had no idea what he was doing apart from trying to warm her up. He suddenly remembered the story of Sleeping Beauty, and how the prince had leaned over, claimed the lips of the beautiful, sleeping maiden and awakened her. It was an absurd urge, a fairy tale, but Mac was exhausted beyond rational thought.

Leaning down once more, Mac placed his lips against Ellie's. Again he was struck by how cool she was. How many times had he wanted to kiss her? To feel the pliancy, the softness of her mouth beneath his? Mac took her lips gently, breathing his life, his love into her with that single, moving gesture.

Ellie felt heat rushing through her, warm, living energy once again being given to her. She was in a dark abyss of nowhere, floating, out of her physical body. But then an incredible heat, a life-giving heat, began to flow through her; it was as if someone was literally breathing life back into her. She moved out of the darkness, into gray light, and then, very slowly, Ellie became aware of a strong, cherished mouth upon her lips. Somehow, she knew it was Mac.

As it lifted, she felt bereft, but somewhat stronger. Her mind was spongy, though, and not working properly. Her senses were shorted out, but she was vaguely aware of a warm pair of hands holding her chilled fingers. They were Mac's. They had to be. An incredible sense of love swept up through Ellie. How could she have doubted her feelings for him? Hadn't he accepted her on every level?

Ellie stopped struggling, because she knew she had to conserve what glimmer of life energy she had. With every passing minute, she became more and more aware of Mac, of his strong, warm touch. Other sounds began to infiltrate her awareness, other voices, and finally, the smells that told her she was in a hospital of some kind. But where? Ellie tried to recall what had happened, but couldn't. It took too much effort.

Mac's heart began to pound when he saw Ellie's lashes move. And then she opened her lips, as if to speak.

"Dr. Johnson!" he called, his voice rolling through the dispensary. Ellie was regaining consciousness! Thrilled but apprehensive, he moved closer and placed his other hand on the crown of Ellie's head.

"It's okay, Ellie. You're safe, and everything's all right." It wasn't, but the possibility sounded good to Mac. He saw her lashes move again, and he smiled a little. "That's it, come back to me, Ellie. Come home, sweetheart. I'm here. I'll take care of you...." He was speaking softly because he didn't want the dispensary personnel to overhear him.

For the next ten minutes, Ellie drifted in and out of consciousness. She heard Mac talking urgently to the doctor, and felt the steadying strength of his hand around hers. She felt other, professional hands on her, taking her blood pressure, examining her. Finally she was able to gather what little strength she had to open her eyes.

Her vision was blurred at first, but she recognized Mac's tall, strong body and the shape of his face. She blinked slowly, and her eyes gradually cleared. She felt Mac's hand tighten around hers.

"Ellie?"

Tears pricked her lids. Mac's voice was hoarse with feeling. "Y-yes." It was such an effort to speak. She moved her chapped, dry lips, but no more sounds would come.

Mac leaned down, his ear close to her lips. "What is it, Ellie? Please, talk to me. Talk."

"Home," she finally got out with a monumental effort. "Take me home...."

"Impossible," Dr. Johnson said as she put the blood-pressure cuff aside. "Ms. O'Gentry's blood pressure is still low."

"But not in the danger zone, as before?" Mac demanded, straightening.

"No, it's rising slowly."

Ellie tried to focus on Mac's voice; she couldn't keep her eyes open. He never stopped holding her hand, and that alone told her so much. Despite her lethargy, her bodily weakness, she felt his protective stance toward her and heard the agitation in his voice when he spoke.

"I'm going to take her home, Doctor."

"That's impossible! We haven't gotten the results back from the lab yet, Major."

Mac glanced down at Ellie. Her face had taken on a bit more color. For the first time, he felt a weak response in her fingers. That settled it. He held the doctor's challenging gaze.

"I'm taking her home. You can contact me there. I'll be staying with her until she recovers."

"Really, Major, I think you are jeopardizing the patient."

Mac shook his head. Something told him to get Ellie home, that she would recover more quickly in her own environment. "Sorry, Doc, but I'm taking her out of here. I'll go sign the release forms and you can call me with the lab results."

Dr. Johnson scowled, then shrugged. "I'll call you as soon as the lab reports come in, Major Stanford."

Mac was grateful that the doctor had given in gracefully. He glanced down at Ellie and saw that her eyes were open. To his alarm, he saw no life in them, only darkness. Giving her his full attention, he leaned over the gurney, his hand resting gently against her head.

"Ellie? Can you hear me?"

She nodded and slowly licked her dry lips. Mac's touch alone was stabilizing in a new and wonderful way to her. "Mac, just get me home. All I need is rest—and sleep. Please?"

He smiled uncertainly. "You got it, sweetheart." He wanted to lean over and kiss her, but censored the idea. There was darkness in Ellie's eyes, along with something else that scared him badly. "You're getting out of here if I have to carry you." And then his smile broadened a bit. "I carried you in. I guess I can carry you out."

Ellie closed her eyes, sagging in relief. She didn't remember Mac carrying her anywhere. She didn't want him to know how close to dying she had come. Right now, her vital functions were barely above survival level and Ellie knew it. She also knew that nothing in a hospital would help her. The damage she'd sustained in the attack had injured her aura, something hospitals and doctors wouldn't acknowledge as part of her being.

Later, she felt herself being lifted off the gurney. Mac's voice was soothing and reassuring, and she remembered little except nestling her head against his shoulder as he carried her out of the antiseptic-smelling hospital into the warmth of morning sunlight. Ellie was too weak to even try to lift her lashes to see the world around her as he drove her home. All she focused on was Mac's hand over hers as he rested it against his long, hard thigh. It was enough.

Ellie moved slowly, feeling drugged from sleep. She was covered with several blankets, and she could smell the fresh scent of cotton encasing the pillow where her head rested. Blinking her eyes, she realized that she was in her own bedroom. The gray light of dusk filtered through the sheer, pale green curtains at the window. Her senses were sluggish. Someone stirred to her left, and she slowly rolled over onto her back. Mac was sitting in the rocking chair in the corner, studying her intently.

"How are you doing?" he asked, quickly moving to her side. He sat down on the edge of the mattress and faced her. Ellie's skin was now nearly a normal color, and her eyes had some life in them. Relief jagged through him. He reached out, grazing her cheek with his fingers. Her skin was now warm instead of cool.

Mac's touch was like a balm to her shattered soul. Ellie closed her eyes momentarily, absorbing his feather-light touch. "Better," she croaked. And then she forced her eyes open. "I'm so thirsty Mac...."

"I figured you would be. Hold on, I made some orange juice. It's in the refrigerator." He got to his feet and gave her a brief smile. "I'll get you some."

Grateful beyond words, Ellie watched him exit the room quietly. She heard the stereo on in the living room, the music soft and soothing. Looking slowly around, Ellie forced herself up into a sitting position.

How weak she was! She was trembling from that small amount of exertion. She took in a long, unsteady breath of air. Now, as never before, she realized how close she'd come to dying in that hangar last night.

Mac reappeared, and she looked up, pinned beneath his warm, worried look as he sat back down on the bed. "Are you up to holding this glass?"

"I—I don't think so...." Her voice sounded gravelly from disuse. Ellie raised her hands, her fingers draping around Mac's as he held the glass steady for her. She sipped the cool, sweet liquid until nearly half the contents were gone.

"Thank you."

Mac set the glass on the bedstand and watched Ellie closely. "Are you hungry?"

She shook her head. "No. I feel like I got run over by a bulldozer."

It was a poor joke, but Mac smiled tentatively and took her hand. "This has been the longest day of my life, Ellie."

Meeting his gaze, she nodded. "I know. I'm sorry, Mac. I didn't realize how powerful that entity was." She squeezed his hand weakly. "I didn't mean to put you in danger. I never thought it would attack you."

"What?"

She licked her lips slowly, her mind barely functioning. Ellie realized that Mac had undressed her and put her in a fresh cotton nightgown. She was too exhausted to feel any embarrassment, grateful for his remaining with her throughout the day.

"The entity attacked you first." She gazed into his troubled eyes, which were ringed with fatigue. Had Mac slept at all? Ellie didn't think so.

"How?"

"Didn't you feel it? He hit you in the heart chakra—in the center of your chest—and tried to stop your heart from beating."

Mac's brows fell. He continued to gently run his thumb across the top of Ellie's hand. "Was that it? I was out of breath. I felt like someone had taken a sixteen-pound sledgehammer to my chest."

"Exactly." Grimacing, Ellie felt some of her strength return. She didn't know whether it was the orange juice or Mac's presence. Probably both.

"I didn't know I was being attacked." Mac shook his head and stared into her exhausted eyes. "At first, I thought it was my imagination. I thought I was imagining it because I was worried for you."

"No, he went after you," Ellie said painfully.

"Why?"

"Because you weren't protected like I was. He's an awful spirit, Mac. He was smart—he knew if he could put you out of commission and prevent you from drumming, I couldn't get to him." Worriedly, Ellie reached out, cupping her hand against the dark growth of beard on Mac's cheek. It was obvious he hadn't shaved; his hair was a bit ruffled, and he was wearing the same clothes as yesterday. Mac had put her before himself, and that touched Ellie as nothing else could.

"I see that look in your eyes," Mac whispered, placing his hand against hers. The tingle of pleasure he felt from her hand pressed to his cheek radiated outward, and he ached to lean those last few inches and kiss her. He wondered if Ellie recalled his kissing her. "I'm okay, sweetheart. I survived, and more important, you will, too."

"I just feel so badly," Ellie said, tears coming to her eyes. "I've never dealt with a spirit like this. I've been attacked before, but not at this level of intensity."

With a sigh, Mac nodded. "You scared the hell out of me, Ellie. When you went pale and slumped down on that chair, I thought you'd died. I stopped drumming and made a grab for you before you fell to the concrete." He took her hand and kissed the back of it. "I felt so damn helpless. You were unconscious, and all I could think to do was get you to the nearest medical facility—the dispensary on base. I lied to them. I told them you were in the car with me and suddenly lost consciousness."

Ellie's lips parted and she whispered Mac's name. "What got me in trouble was that I jumped between you and the entity in order to protect you. My spirit guides normally do the protecting, while I stand back out of the way and remain safe. They're like a shield— they prevent me from being hurt." With a shrug, Ellie said, "When I realized it was attacking you, I forgot. I forgot to stay out of it and let them do the work." Shyly, she looked up into his dark, burning eyes. "I was so scared of losing you, Mac. I—I know it sounds silly. We haven't known each other that long, but I put myself between you and the spirit and took the next blow." She shuddered. "If I hadn't, you might be dead...."

Shaken, Mac placed his hands on her slumped shoulders. "Look at me," he rasped, placing his finger beneath her chin. As Ellie lifted her lashes, he saw that her eyes were bright with tears. His mouth moved into a tender smile. "I found out something last night, too. I found out how very much you mean to me, Ellie—shamanism and all. When you were on the floor, out cold, all I could think of was that I'd never have another hour with you. We'd never get to hold each other when we danced. Never share a cup of coffee on that bench out back in your garden. Never—" He choked, unable to go on. Tears drifted down her cheeks, and he felt tears of his own in his eyes.

Without a word, Mac drew Ellie forward and leaned down, capturing her mouth. This time she was awake. This time she was warm, alive and responsive to his tender, searching kiss. Her mouth was like a lush blossom opening beneath the questing sun, only he was the sun, her light, her life. Sliding his hands upward, framing her face, he drank deeply of her, of the life that she offered and surrendered to him. Their breathing was ragged, but synchronous. He felt Ellie tremble as he worshipped her mouth with reverence. Her hands slid around his shoulders and came to rest against his neck, her fingers threading through the short strands of his hair. Never had anything seemed so right to Mac, so rich, so simple and yet powerful.

Time ebbed to a halt, a spinning heat enveloping Ellie as he kissed her deeply, exploring her as if she were some fragile flower that might suddenly crumple and be destroyed. He tasted of coffee, and of sunlight. His hands were strong, cherishing and steadying. His mouth was tender; she could feel him holding back, not wanting to take her hard and fast, but to savor her like a precious glass of wine.

Ellie felt beautiful in a new and surprising way. Mac's touch, his fingers tunneling through her hair, his mouth cajoling, his arms holding her close, converged in a symphony of sight, sound, texture and taste. She never wanted the kiss to end, but she also felt Mac's powerful need ready to overwhelm the tight controls he had placed on himself for her benefit. Ellie had no reason to embarrass him in that way, and reluctantly eased her lips from his mouth.

"You're sweet," Mac whispered roughly, kissing her cheek, brow and hair, "like honey. Hot, sweet honey." He slid his fingers through her loose, thick hair of shimmering ebony silk. He couldn't get enough of Ellie—he needed to touch her, taste her, inhale her. Mac wanted her to realize he loved her from the depths of his battered heart. He knew he wasn't the best catch in the world, but he would give anything for a chance with this special woman. How he yearned to be an important part of her life!

All those feelings, those needs, coursed through him in moments. He saw the dazed, lustrous look in Ellie's dark eyes. In their depths he saw the first sparks of life—she was truly on the mend. Relief, sharp and serrating, overrode his other emotions. He framed her face with his hands and looked deep into her eyes.

"You're so important to me, Ellie. More important than any job. More important than flying. Do you understand that?"

A quiver of fear ran through Ellie as she stared up at Mac. The sincerity coming from his generous heart was unquestionable. She drew in a ragged breath. "I'm so afraid, Mac. So afraid...."

"I know you are," he rasped. He kissed her brow. "Let's both be scared, then. Me, of losing you, and you, of wanting me as much as I want you."

Ellie nodded, lost in the heat of his gaze, in the beauty of his desire for her, which went far beyond the physical realm. "Just be patient with me, Mac. Please...."

His smile was gentle. "Sweetheart, you can have all the time in the world. I'm in no hurry." That was a lie, but Ellie had to realize that she was the one in control of their escalating relationship. Mac knew she cared a great deal for him or she'd never have placed herself in that kind of danger for him. Her act of protection was akin to a person throwing herself in front of a car to save another, and he knew it. There were no medals for Ellie, for what she'd done to protect him. But he'd remember.

"I'm so tired, Mac. I'm sorry, but I just can't seem to stay awake anymore."

"I understand." He eased off the bed and allowed Ellie to lie back down. He tucked the sheet and blanket around her shoulders. "Get some sleep."

Tiredly, she nodded. "Listen, you don't have to stay. I know you've probably been up all night and you're exhausted, too."

He placed his hands on his hips and smiled down at her. "I saw you had a guest bedroom, so I'm going to make myself something to eat, shower and crash there. If you need anything, you let me know."

She held out her hand to him and he grasped it. "Thank you, Mac. You're so very special. Thank you...."

CHAPTER TEN

Ellie awoke slowly, the fragrance of frying bacon bringing her out of the deep, healing sleep. What time was it? She forced her lashes up and groggily looked at the clock on the nightstand. It was eight a.m.! Normally, she rose at five-thirty every morning. She lay very still, taking inventory of how she felt mentally, emotionally and physically. Surprisingly, she felt strong, very strong. Had it been because of the kiss Mac had shared with her last night?

No longer doubting what her heart knew, Ellie eased into a sitting position, the sheet and blankets pooling around her waist. The bacon smelled good and she was hungry. In fact, she was starving. Getting out of bed, Ellie slipped into her white, ankle-length chenille robe. Her hair was in utter disarray, and she tamed some of the strands away from her face.

After finishing her toilette, Ellie wandered down the hall toward the kitchen. Mac had stayed the night in the other room, and she had to admit a large part of her had wanted him in her bed—with her. She halted at the entrance to the kitchen.

Mac was dressed in a pair of Levi's and a blue plaid, short-sleeved shirt; his beard was gone and his hair had been recently washed. He was busy with the bacon and didn't hear her approach. How wonderful he looked! Ellie felt her heart lurch with such an over-powering river of emotions that she could only stand there and feel them.

Mac's face was utterly relaxed, his mouth no longer in that thin line that indicated he was holding back a lot of feelings. Even his hair mirrored his casual state, a few strands dipping boyishly across his brow. Serenity and peace permeated the kitchen.

Far different from yesterday, Ellie thought ruefully. Finally she stepped into the kitchen.

"Have you traded in your job as an eagle to become a beaver?"

Mac turned at Ellie's husky voice. He smiled a little and put the rest of the fried bacon into the basket.

"I don't know about a beaver—I feel more like a bull in a china shop."

She smiled softly and moved toward Mac. He set the skillet aside and turned to meet her. She wasn't disappointed as his hands settled on her shoulders and he drew her against him. Automatically, her arms went around his waist. How wonderful it was to be able to rest her cheek against his chest and hear the slow, unfettered pounding of his heart beneath his shirt. She sighed as Mac moved one hand up and down her spine, stroking her. Ellie knew that he loved her. It was in his eyes, in his touch, and in the way his voice had changed to that intimate, caring tone after she had been injured by the entity's attack.

The words *I love you* almost slipped from her lips as she nestled her cheek against his chest and surrendered to his care. It was too soon. Ellie's mind once again got in the way, warning her that if she tried to love Mac in return, that someday, somehow, he would turn against her—just as Brian had. It would only be a matter of time....

"You look like you'll live," Mac observed, pressing a small, chaste kiss against her temple, the silky strands of her hair beneath his lips.

"I will," Ellie murmured. She eased out of his arms enough to lift her head and drown in his green-and-gold eyes. There was such love in them that it nearly brought tears to her own. Swallowing the sudden lump in her throat, Ellie added, "I'm fine now. Really."

"I see life in your eyes." The gold, dancing sunlight was there once more, and he breathed in deeply, grateful that Ellie was truly all right.

"Last night," he whispered, "I dreamed I was holding you."

"We must have sharing the same dream."

Mac stopped himself from saying too much too soon. It was a lot for her to accept this much intimacy from him. With a slight smile, he said, "I got up a couple of times last night and checked on you. Before the dream of holding you, I kept waking up with nightmares of you dying."

Touched, Ellie caressed Mac's cheek. "I'm sorry I had to put you through this."

"I'm not complaining, sweetheart." Mac captured a long, ebony strand of her hair. "It's a part of your life."

Ellie searched his hooded gaze for some telltale sign that he wasn't being completely honest with himself, but she found nothing to indicate that. "Things like this are rare. They hardly ever happen, Mac."

"That's the good news," he said wryly as he released her. "Are you hungry?"

"Starving."

"Is that normal after a psychic attack?"

"Yes." She took the chair he pulled out for her. As she sat down, she noticed Mac had cut some of her roses and made a pretty arrangement in a vase. Again, she was struck by his sensitivity, his knowing instinctively what made her happy. Her ex-husband had never once put flowers in a vase—either on the table or anywhere else. Flowers weren't in his vocabulary. But then, Ellie reminded herself, her ex-husband wasn't a man of the earth. Neither was Mac, but at least he understood her needs, her own love of the earth.

Mac moved to the oven and opened it. "I took the liberty of making my favorite breakfast—scrambled eggs mixed with cream cheese and bacon bits." Proudly, he placed two plates on the table and brought over the basket of fried bacon. Then he brought over cups of hot coffee and sat down opposite Ellie, who was smiling.

"I didn't realize you had this hausfrau streak in you." She added three strips of bacon to the egg concoction on her plate.

"Necessity is the mother of invention. When I got divorced, it was either cook or starve to death. I don't like junk food and got tired of eating plastic breakfast at fast-food chains." Mac dug hungrily into his own food.

"This is good." She grinned a little. "You have hidden talents, Major. I'm impressed."

"Don't be. I've got about ten recipes and then things go to hell in a hand basket."

"At least you can boil water."

Chuckling, Mac nodded. After a few moments, he got serious. "Yesterday morning I called my master sergeant and told him to take my squadron crews to Hangar 12. I've shut down 13, Ellie, until I know what to do with it. I also called the colonel and told him I wouldn't be coming in today, either." He shrugged. "After what happened I'm not about to let any of my people walk unsuspecting into that hangar."

"You did the right thing, Mac."

He shook his head. "I just wouldn't have believed it, Ellie, if I hadn't experienced the whole thing." He frowned. "I'm sorry I doubted you."

"Don't be hard on yourself, Mac. Most people would react the same way."

"You're very generous with your understanding of the rest of us."

Ellie took a sip of coffee. How very right it seemed for Mac to be here, in her kitchen. She'd never had a man make her breakfast before, and it was a pleasurable treat, completely unexpected. "Over the years I learned to be patient with other people's attitudes. I don't blame people for disbelieving in metaphysics. How can you prove the unseen? There's no machine that measures the other dimensions."

"I didn't need a machine to prove it to me the other night," he growled.

"Now you're a true believer," Ellie said with a smile. "It always happens that way. When a person has some psychic experience, he finally opens up and believes in the unseen. That's the way it will be until we get those sensitive machines to prove it to the rest of the world.''

With a shake of his head, Mac finished his eggs. ''I was thinking this morning that if I hadn't met you, hadn't been brought up to speed on what was happening in Hangar 13, I wouldn't have known what else to do, to try.''

''I know.'' Ellie put her plate aside, half empty. ''I did manage to talk to the spirit, Mac. He gave me the name of his killer.''

''Oh?'' Mac picked up his coffee.

Ellie related what had happened. When she finished, she said, ''At least you've got the name of the man who accidentally killed him.''

Mac nodded. ''It's a good lead. I'll call the provost marshal's office and get them to run the information, to verify that Treadwell exists.''

''Good.'' Ellie sat back. ''That still doesn't solve the problem, though.''

''What do you mean?''

She stood up and leaned against the kitchen counter. ''The entity called his killing a murder. But it sounded like an accident to me. The man pushed him and he slipped and hit his head.''

''Okay...''

She opened her hands. ''I'm afraid the entity won't leave even if we do catch the culprit responsible for his death.''

Mac rubbed his jaw. ''Why not?''

''He's been drawing on any unsuspecting human being who has crossed his path for many years, ever since his death. He's accumulated a great deal of energy—more than enough to live on. His firepower, if you will, is massive. We both got a taste of that the other night."

Mac nodded. "So where does that leave us? He nearly killed you. Dr. Johnson was alarmed at how low your blood pressure fell. You could have gone into cardiac arrest."

"I don't have enough power to wrestle successfully with this entity, Mac."

"I figured that. So how can we get it out of the hangar? How can I protect my crews?"

She liked Mac's ability to say "we," as if it wasn't solely her problem. But it was. "I'm convinced the entity can't be talked out of leaving. When I asked him if I could help him get back the missing pieces of his soul, which would automatically release him and make him go into the light, he refused. All he wants is vengeance, Mac."

"I'm not going to let you go back in there, Ellie," he said in a low voice. "It almost killed you." He came over to the counter where she stood and put his hands on her shoulders. "This is *our* problem, and I'm not asking you to personally put yourself in the line of fire again."

"Line of fire is a good analogy," Ellie admitted quietly. In the back of her mind, she wondered why Johanna hadn't been able to appreciate Mac's natural warmth and sensitivity. Placing her hands on his waist, she looked up at his dark, worried face. "One thing I learned a long time ago, Mac, was to respect my abilities—and their limitations. A shaman can be overwhelmed and possibly killed if he isn't smart enough to know when he's lacking and back off."

"Good," he said, relief in his voice. "I was afraid you'd march right back in there and take on the entity by yourself again." His hands tightened briefly on Ellie's shoulders. She was so strong, yet so soft.

"I'm not stupid, Mac. Being a shamaness always keeps you humble, believe me. I'm constantly shown where my weaknesses are, and where I need to work in order to turn them into strengths."

"How can you deal with this entity, then?"

"What do you know about Native American pipes?"

He shrugged. "Peace pipes?"

"Yes, sort of...."

Mac released her and took her hand. "Come on, let's go sit out in your flower garden and talk."

Ellie nodded and fell into step with him. How had he known she wanted to go outside? She chalked it up to the natural mental telepathy that existed between people who were close—a mother with her child, a lover with his woman.

The sun was rising in the east as Ellie and Mac sat down on the redwood bench. Ellie looked lovingly at the profusion of rosebushes now blooming with fragrant flowers. The honeysuckle that climbed the walls had broken out in small white-and-yellow flowers that scented the small compound. The temperature was in the low seventies, and perfect.

Ellie gathered her thoughts for a moment. "My mother is a ceremonial and personal pipe carrier for our Cherokee nation, Mac. Pipes have been with us for over a hundred thousand years—that's the story that's been passed down to us, at least, through many of the clans. Pipes are a sacred way to conduct and pray to the Great Spirit, or God. There's more to them than just smoking them.''

She rested her elbows on her thighs, her gaze fixed on the roses against the opposite wall. "Normally, we never speak about the pipes because they are so sacred." She glanced at Mac's serious features.

"I see. So they're used for only special occasions?''

"That's right. You know, ceremony is very powerful in and of itself—even without a pipe. I've been taught ceremonies by my mother that are thousands of years old.'' She straightened and picked up a small stick. Bending over, she drew a circle in the sand. "Let's say this circle symbolizes a particular ceremony. What you need to grasp is that every time that ceremony is performed from the heart, with good, pure intent and prayer, it becomes a key that unlocks an invisible door in the other dimensions.

"When a person performs this ceremony, making all the right gestures, singing the correct songs in correct order, or moving physically in a certain direction, all this intent and physical movement is translated into a key. That key then opens the door to a huge, archetypal energy. When that happens, the energy flows through the dimension, flows into the ceremony.... It's like unleashing a huge flood.

"When a pipe is used, it intensifies the process a hundredfold. I was taught that the pipe is sacred, and that if you approach it in the correct manner, it, too,

becomes a key. Only this key is a direct line to the
Great Spirit. The pipe acts as a person knocking on the
Great Spirit's door, so to speak, and asking for help.
If the pipe carrier is of good heart, has pure, positive
intent and love, the Great Spirit always responds. The
energy is then released and flows through the pipe and
the pipe carrier to embellish the ceremony."

Mac nodded. "So the pipe," he said, struggling
with the concept, "is a second key that opens up a
second dam of energy?"

"Exactly!" Ellie smiled, pleased. "The ceremony
itself opens up an energy waterfall. But the pipe, if
used in conjunction with it, gives us a second, more
powerful surge of energy from a completely new
source. The Great Spirit is pure love, Mac. It is light.
That is why a pipe carrier is so carefully chosen in the
first place. In the wrong hands, that same energy can
be used for selfish purposes. There are even pipes that
are so powerful and old that their energy can kill if
they fall into the wrong hands. That's why our people
are careful about who they choose to carry a pipe."

"It's like carrying a loaded weapon," Mac observed. "It sounds as though the pipe is a neutral being and that the energy it releases either becomes good
or bad, depending upon the carrier's intent."

"You've got it," Ellie said, congratulating him.
"Nowadays, pipes are given to anyone who wants
them, but most people don't know what to do with
them, or they know only part of the ceremony to 'open
up' a pipe and use it properly. That's why Native
Americans are so upset with whites who want to become 'pseudo-Indian.' To understand ceremony takes

years of preparation, years of instruction, and performing a ceremony without proper knowledge can be terribly dangerous and destructive."

He held her gaze. "You're a pipe carrier? Is that what you're telling me?"

"Yes, I am. But I'm only a personal pipe carrier, not a ceremonial one. In order to carry a ceremonial pipe, as my mother does, you have to be from a certain clan lineage. You also have to be a medicine person who is highly regarded and trusted. Ceremonial pipe carriers live on the reservation and are charged with maintaining the sacred energy of the Cherokee people. They must be of pure heart and moral in all ways. That's not to say they're perfect, but they're always striving to evolve spiritually to a higher plane of goodness, of love."

Impressed, Mac asked, "And how do you become a personal pipe carrier?"

"There is a group within the clans who look for good candidates." Ellie touched her robe above her heart. "They look for a person who is morally upstanding, who has care and concern for others rather than himself and who will be a good role model for the children. In the old days, pipe carriers were the most respected of all, Mac. They were usually elders in the tribe before they were given the honor of carrying a personal pipe. And they had earned them. They always helped others and clearly understood the relationship between self, family and clans—that without that generosity of spirit and self, the entire fabric would be destroyed." She smiled a little. "That was then. Nowadays, there are a number of Cherokee men and women all over the world who are personal pipe carriers."

"But you practice what you preach, no matter where you are."

"Yes. Part of being a pipe carrier is possessing humility. You would never hear me mention that I was a pipe carrier if this problem with the entity hadn't come up. To tell others you carry a pipe is bragging. It isn't proper for a pipe carrier to have such a negative trait."

"I see." He slowly rubbed his hands together between his opened thighs. "So what you're leading up to is that with a certain ceremony and the pipe you carry, you can get rid of that entity?"

With a sigh, Ellie nodded. "Maybe."

"What do you mean?"

"The pipe I carry is a young one. We have pipes among the people that are hundreds of years old, Mac. The older a pipe is, the more powerful it becomes. My pipe is only ten years old."

"Are pipes passed on from one generation to another? It sounds like it."

"Yes, they are. And as they are used and passed on, they become older and more powerful. That's why—" Ellie glanced up at him "—the Cherokee people hide their old pipes. There are white people, even Indians, who want to steal them—we call them power stalkers. We have renegades among our own kind who would do anything, even kill, to get hold of these older pipes. My mother has a special hiding place for the Wolf Clan ceremonial pipe and she's never revealed it to anyone, for fear that one of us might slip someday and let it be known to the wrong party."

"Interesting," Mac observed. "So this pipe of yours—do you feel it can help us?"

She nodded. "I hope so. I'm going to have to go back to that hangar tonight. I'll perform the spirit-releasing ceremony and smoke the pipe on behalf of the entity. If it goes well, the entity will be forced to leave. He'll have to move out of the hangar, and will become suspended in another dimension until he's ready to receive his pieces back as well as give back the pieces he's taken from others.

"I have to be in a very special place within my heart and soul to do this ceremony. One slip, any loss of concentration and focus, and I'm opening myself up again to his attack." She didn't add, *and this time, he could kill me.* Mac didn't need to know that. She didn't want to worry him any more than necessary.

Mac looked at her, his eyes grim, his expression apprehensive. "I want to be there with you."

"No." She shook her head and rose to her feet. "There's no sense in putting two of us in jeopardy, Mac."

"But don't you need the drum beaten?"

"Not for this. I'm not going into an altered state this time. I'll be fully in my body, fully here in the third dimension when I perform the ceremony. That is part of my protection—being in my body."

Concerned, Mac reached out, his hand resting on her shoulder. "I'm not letting you go in there alone, Ellie. You mean too much to me—" He bit back the rest of what he was going to say. She looked so serene when he felt so agitated and worried.

"I know, Mac, and I feel the same way," she whispered. "But I have to go alone. That's part of the pipe carrier's mission in life, you see. We are learning to walk alone, in the grace and love of the Great Spirit's protection, guidance and care. If you are there, my focus may be altered. I can't risk it. I can't risk that the entity might attack you first."

Mac shook his head. "No way, Ellie. I'm not letting you handle this thing alone. I grant that I'm not a pipe carrier and I don't know anything about ceremony, but I'm not leaving you alone to that thing in there."

She felt the tremendous warmth of his care, his love. "Okay," she began hesitantly, "there's only one way I'll allow you to be there, to be with me."

"Tell me."

"I can put you in the circle. There's protection there. The entity will know as I lay down the sacred cornmeal that he can't attack us if we're in that circle."

"But it's not guaranteed?"

"Yes, it will be. I just don't want him to attack me before I'm prepared for him." She gave him a searching look. "Mac, you've got to realize that if you move, if you sneeze, cough or do *anything,* it can throw off my concentration, my focus."

"I won't move," he promised her thickly. "I would never put you in danger, Ellie."

"Not willingly," she conceded softly, "but you're a human being. What if you suddenly have to sneeze?"

"Listen to me," he said, gripping her shoulders and giving her a small shake, "I'm a fighter pilot. When my adrenaline is flowing, I have control over my physical body. When I'm scared, Ellie, my body doesn't betray me. I'm scared for you. I'm scared to death, if you want the truth, but I'm not going to put you in danger. Do you understand?"

She did. "I'm scared, too, Mac. Scared for both of us. I've never had to resort to a pipe-release ceremony to get a spirit to move on. A journey has always been enough."

"Not this time." Mac met her sad eyes. "And you're not doing this alone, Ellie."

"Okay..." she whispered defeatedly, though she hated the idea. Mac was simply not prepared for this entity.

Releasing her, Mac took her hand. "I'm worried about your energy. Do you feel up to this tonight, Ellie?"

She didn't, but she also knew that he would be forced to allow his people back into that hangar sooner or later. She had to attempt the release as soon as possible, for everyone's safety.

"I'm up to it," she lied.

Unconvinced, Mac studied her in the ensuing silence. "My gut tells me you aren't sure."

Forcing a smile for his benefit, Ellie said, "I'll rest up today in preparation for the ceremony tonight."

"Do you want me to stay?"

A huge part of her did, but Mac was a distraction to her heart, and right now, Ellie had to become very still and balanced within herself. "You can go home. If you want, we can have dinner together tonight."

Hope sprang strongly in him. "How about if I make one of my ten recipes? I'll come over with dinner."

"That sounds wonderful." And it did.

CHAPTER ELEVEN

Ellie tried to calm herself on the way over to the hangar. It was nearly three a.m. The stars in the sky were bright and sparkling, the darkness of the desert bringing out their beauty. Mac drove in silence, his eyes on the road ahead that would take them to the air force base. Ordinarily, Ellie would be swayed by the beauty of the starry night, invigorated by the coolness after the hundred-degree heat of the day, but not tonight.

She wiped her damp palms on her thighs. Her mind was focused on the ceremony she would perform; to miss one facet of it, or to perform it out of order, could place her and Mac in terrible jeopardy. Part of their safety net was the ceremony itself. Her fear of making some mistake filled her body with tension.

The lights of the guard gate appeared, and Ellie blinked. Her heart began to beat faster. Would the entity attack them as they walked into the hangar? If it did, Ellie knew it would be a life-and-death struggle. She prayed that the spirit would wait until she was ready to face him.

Mac parked the car outside Hangar 13 and turned to Ellie. The serious look in her eyes, the grim set of her mouth told him just how dangerous this was going to be.

"If someone had told me a couple of months ago that I'd be working with a shamaness and battling a spirit, I'd have laughed my head off." He reached over and captured one of Ellie's hands. He felt the tension in her and tried to smile. "But I'm not laughing now."

"Because you've had enough proof, Mac, to know that it's as real as you and I."

He nodded and held her worried gaze. "I'd never have believed it," he agreed. "How are you feeling?"

"Scared to death."

"A healthy response."

"I think so."

"It reminds me of going into combat, only this time the enemy is a spirit, not a pilot."

Ellie squeezed his hand. How badly she wanted her life to continue after this night, after this ceremony. But would it? "Mac, I have a request of you," she began hesitantly.

"Sure. What is it?"

Looking away, she stared at the large hangar. "If, by some chance, I'm hurt, or something happens, will you call my mother?" She dug a piece of paper from the pocket of her white cotton skirt. When she handed it to him, she saw his eyes go wide with surprise—and fear. "I—I don't think anything will happen to me, Mac, but just in case. Please?"

He took the carefully folded paper. "Call your mother?" he croaked.

"Yes. I talked to her this afternoon, before you came over with dinner, and I told her what was going on. She agreed with me that the entity is too powerful for me to deal with in normal shamanistic ways, and that the releasing ceremony is the only hope we have of getting it to go on its way and leave people alone.''

He stared at the paper. "I see."

"No, I don't think you do. Mom will be praying for me, as will my sister, Diana. Prayer is very powerful, Mac. Much more so than most people give it credit for. It doesn't matter whether you're praying to Buddha, God or the Great Spirit—the prayers are heard.

"If—if something goes wrong, if I make a mistake during the ceremony, I want you to realize that the entity will probably attack me. He can't attack as long as I am in the stream of energy flowing through that open door from the other dimensions. But if I miss something by accident, then I'm wide open."

Mac nodded. "I see."

"This time," she whispered, her voice husky with emotion, "I may not come out of it, Mac. I told my mother everything, and she agreed that I need to get rid of this entity now, before it becomes even more powerful and starts attacking people outside the hangar. I...it's my battle, my problem. They will pray for me, and that is protection in and of itself."

Mac felt her terror, and it shook him as nothing else could. Putting the paper in his shirt pocket, he placed his hands on her shoulders. "Ellie, we're going to get through this together. We're *both* going to be safe. Do you understand that? You're not going to mess up on this ceremony." He stared into her shadowed eyes. "I know you're scared. So am I. We'll be scared together."

His hands tightened on her shoulders. "Sweetheart, I want the rest of my lifetime to get to know you. I'll be damned if some entity is going to stop my dream by hurting you. I know I'm new to this world of yours, but I've got faith. Faith in you, in the process. You come from a family who have their hearts in the right place—you have a strong heritage to back up your skills. Most of all, you have the courage and the spirit to get this done."

She sighed. "My mother told me this afternoon that it was a test."

"A test?" Mac snorted. "What is this? Some kind of game?"

"No," Ellie said quickly, "it's never a game, Mac. But people who work in this are tested from time to time. It's not a bad thing. You get tested, don't you, as a pilot?"

Grudgingly, Mac nodded. "Yes."

"And sometimes those tests are life-and-death situations, aren't they?"

"Sometimes," he answered heavily.

"My world is no different than yours, Mac. Instead of an enemy pilot who can fire rockets at me, I have to face an entity that has too much power for its own good. I'm charged with trying to protect the innocent people who may be harmed by him, just as you are charged with protecting civilians from that enemy pilot."

Mac saw the wisdom of her example. "It's just that the enemy aircraft is real, Ellie. I can lock on target and shoot him out of the sky." He glanced at the hangar and back at her. "You can't fight this entity the same way."

"No, we fight it with love, Mac. I have to have enough faith and trust in the Great Spirit and open my heart fully to this malevolent entity. In that way, we are different. There is no love involved when you fire on an enemy aircraft."

"How can you love that thing?"

She smiled a little. "The Red Road, our way of life as Native Americans, has taught us to speak from our heart at all times, Mac. I'm not saying we always do it, but we're taught to try, and that is what counts." She gestured to the hangar. "I have great compassion for that entity. He is trapped, he is enraged and he is in great pain."

"And he could kill you."

"Yes. But I'm betting that my love for him is greater than his hatred for me. If I can maintain that openness, Mac, if I can trust fully and completely in the ceremony, then the love will release him." She smiled softly. "Love is like sunlight—it's warm, beautiful, peaceful and freeing."

Reaching over, Mac touched the slope of her cheek. "That's what you are to me, Ellie," he whispered roughly. "All those things."

Feeling heat move into her face, she lowered her lashes. Her cheek tingled beneath his touch, and she wanted to lean forward and kiss Mac. But now was not the time or place. She had to keep her focus on the entity, on the final battle to come.

"What we share," she said, "is new and beautiful."

"Something I want to keep, Ellie. Something I want to explore with you." Mac wanted to add *forever,* but held back the word. "And we will," he said urgently.

Placing her hand on the car door, she said, "It's time, Mac. Let's walk this together."

With a nod, he eased out of the car. His wristwatch read exactly three a.m. High tide in the universe. As he carried Ellie's small suitcase of ceremonial items, he wondered if the higher energy would help get rid of the entity. He felt no love toward it like Ellie did. He wanted it out of the hangar, out of their lives—once and for all. Worry for Ellie seesawed back and forth with his love for her. He felt so damned helpless. There was nothing he could do to help her—or protect her.

At the side door to Hangar 13, Ellie turned to him. She took a necklace she always wore and eased it over her head.

"Here, I want you to wear this, Mac."

It was a long, silver necklace with a large bear claw suspended from it. "Why?" He lowered his head so she could place it around his neck.

"Because," Ellie said softly, settling the bear claw against his heart, "it will protect you. It's bear medicine—one of the most powerful medicines we have to work with."

"But you need it, don't you?"

She shrugged. "My mother used to send me on vision quests once a year, Mac. When you go out on a vision quest, you go out into the wilderness with a pipe, a blanket and some water—and that's it. In the Great Smoky Mountains of our reservation, there're plenty of black bears. We sit within a sacred circle for up to four days, singing, praying and sleeping. In those years many wild and even dangerous animals came up to me. But they never stepped within the sacred circle of my vision quest. The circle I will create here will do the same thing for both of us. The bear claw is added protection for you.''

Ellie entered the hangar then, allowing him no further argument. The gloom in the hangar was pervasive. Mac quietly shut the door and then locked it. Setting Ellie's suitcase down, he turned and watched her.

Ellie's hair felt as if it stood on end. Even now she could feel the presence of the entity, its agitation that they were once again in his hangar. Her heart was pounding hard, almost like a drum in her breast.

"He's agitated," Ellie said softly, keeping her gaze on the opposite corner.

"What do you want me to do?"

Ellie loved Mac fiercely in that moment. He could have said or done many things, but he hadn't; he'd deferred to her needs. "Slowly open the suitcase for me."

Mac quietly set the piece of luggage on its side. He had no idea what was in the case. As he eased the lid upward, he could feel the threat in the hangar. His gut tightened automatically, a sick sense of dread filling him. If he felt this, what must Ellie be feeling?

Concentrate. The word poured through Ellie. She felt a new kind of energy moving through the top of her head, flowing downward through her. It was a powerful energy and it wasn't her own. Grateful that the Great Spirit was helping her, she knew she had to perform her end of the duties. She crouched down over the suitcase, pulling out a deerskin bag filled with the cornmeal that was sacred to her people. It would form the physical circle, the circle that would protect them.

She felt the entity probing, wondering what she was doing. She felt its curiosity, and its fear. Keeping her heart open, feeling compassion for it, Ellie lifted the elk-skin pipe bag onto the crook of her left arm, and cradled it as if it were a much-loved child. It was that and much more. Next came a black pottery bowl and the sacred sage. With all her supplies gathered, she rose.

Without a word, Ellie moved into the gloom, near the center of the hangar. She wore moccasins, so she made no sound. Mac walked behind her, knowing that he must be silent as well. Ellie had warned him to always remain behind her. What she didn't tell him was why—so that if the entity attacked, it would have to go through her first in order to get to him.

Ellie placed the articles on the cool concrete floor, with the exception of the deerskin bag containing the cornmeal. She wished she was more clairvoyant, like her mother, who could not only sense, but see into the other realms without going into an altered state. Right now, Ellie knew she was at a great—and dangerous—disadvantage. She wouldn't really be aware of any charge toward her until it hit her—and then it could be too late.

As Ellie lifted the bag upward, above her head, she spoke a prayer out loud. To say a prayer silently was fine, but during ceremony, it was more powerful to speak the words aloud in the third dimension, for it anchored the energy.

"Great Spirit, I ask your blessing upon this corn-meal, which has given its life so that we may continue to live." As she held the bag up in the gloom, she felt a tingling sensation begin in her fingers, then quickly spread through the bag, down her arm and through all of her body. Closing her eyes, Ellie gave an internal sigh of gratefulness. She had performed this cere-mony many times during the years when she'd lived on the reservation, but she hadn't done one in the last seven years, since moving to Phoenix. She had been afraid that because she was rusty, it wouldn't work. Luckily, she was wrong.

As she opened the bag and dug her fingers into the contents, Ellie reminded herself that intention was the key to everything—whether it was a ceremony or something a person wanted out of life. Her intentions were pure, loving, and so the energy was beginning to flow, giving her a sense of protection.

As she took the first granules into her hand, she felt the entity again. Fear clawed at her. Ellie began to sing a ceremonial song, a song of welcoming the Great Spirit to the gathering, and concentrated on sprin-kling a fine, thin line of yellow cornmeal on the con-crete floor. Her nerves tautened. Once this circle was made, it guaranteed protection.

The entity sensed it. Ellie felt a hot, angry force gathering behind her as she continued to slowly walk and sing. The circle would be about thirty feet in di-ameter when she was finished. A chill shot down her spine. Her hand wavered momentarily. Dryness invaded her throat. Concentrate! She closed her eyes and sang more strongly, keeping her heart open, her compassion in place. She wanted to hurry the completion of the circle, but knew she didn't dare. The energy was pouring through her, into the cornmeal, creating the protection. Right now, she was like an open conduit, the energy flowing through her, not from her. In order for the energy to remain in place, to work for all of them, she had to maintain the pace, not letting her personal fears interrupt. If they did, Ellie knew she could die—and so might Mac.

Never had she wanted more to live. She dug into the deerskin pouch again, a quarter of the circle completed. There was so far to go! Ellie sang more strongly, centering herself within the beauty of the music, of the words that beseeched the Great Spirit to work with her on behalf of the spirit who was tied to Mother Earth.

She felt the entity stalking her, coming closer and closer. Ellie felt a bitter taste in her mouth. A chill again ran along her spine. He was coming, and the circle wasn't complete, their protection wasn't in place. Taking a deep breath, she allowed the energy of the song to flow through her as never before while she continued to sprinkle the cornmeal. Let her get the circle completed. Please, let her get the circle completed. The thought was there, pulling at her concentration. Ellie shook herself mentally. She buried all her fears in the song.

Half the circle was now complete. The entity was coming closer, breathing down the back of her neck, taunting her. He was trying to force her to lose her concentration. Fear made Ellie internalize her focus even more powerfully. She knew that the Great Spirit would help, but it was up to her to carry out her responsibilities. If she faltered, so would the energy from the other dimensions. Too much was at stake. Too much. The thought of Mac galvanized her. She realized that for the first time in her life, she felt truly whole in a beautiful, poignant way.

Her mother had been married to her father for thirty years before he died, and Ellie had seen what a loving marriage could be—if both parties worked at it. She had wanted the same for herself, but after Brian, she had lost hope of ever finding it. Now, Mac had crashed into her life and was offering her another chance. But so much stood in the way....

Ellie froze when she felt a blow on the back of her neck. A coldness spread down her spine. The entity had playfully hit her, with enough force to cause her song to waver. He was playing with her, a cat with a helpless mouse. Well, she wasn't helpless, and she couldn't afford to let anger replace her love for the spirit. She brought the song more powerfully to life within her. The spirit was following her, just outside that line of cornmeal. It couldn't move inside the circle, but it could hang over it, lording over her, teasing her, from just the other side of it.

Sweat popped out on her brow and upper lip. The energy from the blow dissolved, but Ellie knew that, more than ever, she had to remain focused. The entity was just waiting for an opportunity to strike her solidly in the heart chakra, and thereby, stop her physical heart from beating. It couldn't happen!

Three-quarters of the circle was now complete. She felt the entity approach her from behind. A part of her wanted to turn and scream at it. But she fought to remain focused on the song, in the compassion of the moment. Sweat was trickling down her rib cage. Her throat was closing up. No! The entity was sending energy to shut down her throat chakra. Without the song, the ceremony was useless! Struggling frantically, Ellie halted. She closed her eyes, concentrating on her song, the cornmeal bunched in her hand. The entity was there, encircling her neck, sending a chilling energy into her throat and neck region.

Great Spirit, help me! Ellie sent the plea mentally and emotionally. She tensed; the song was being squeezed out of her, as if the entity had encircled her entire torso like a boa constrictor, squeezing the life, the air, out of her body. She began to feel dizzy. Her hand clenched into a fist, the cornmeal within it. Desperately, Ellie flailed around within herself, searching for strength. She couldn't fight this entity on her own. He had her. Perspiration made her face gleam in the low lighting; the song was becoming a mere trickle of itself.

Is this what the Great Spirit wanted? Her death? Suddenly, Ellie realized she'd fallen into the oldest trap of all in a metaphysical sense. Most people were afraid of dying, and a malicious entity often would send into a person's mind the worst fear a human being had—of death. The instant she realized that, Ellie felt air tunnel once again into her mouth and down into her lungs, her chant becoming deeper, more resonant.

Again she was reminded of how frail all human beings were—especially her.

The energy lock around her body began to dissipate. Ellie almost laughed with relief. The spirit was intelligent; he knew how to trigger her fears. But now that she'd realized what he was trying to do, she'd destroyed his hold over her. She felt her neck losing the tension that had inhabited it, her lungs expanding with air once again.

Joy moved through Ellie as she worked to complete the cornmeal circle. Again, she felt the entity stalk her. Only five more feet, and the circle would be complete....

Ellie gasped. She jerked upright, her shoulders thrown back. The entity's hatred overwhelmed her in the attack. Dizzied, she fought for coherency. Somewhere in her confusion, she heard Mac gasp. He knew he couldn't touch her, couldn't in any way involve himself. Blackness danced before her eyes. She felt a horrible, bone-chilling cold seep through her, trying to destroy her focus.

No! No! Ellie mentally clawed for stability. Her song faltered, but she forced the words out of her throat. She must complete the circle! The entity was swirling around her, trying to pound away at her heart chakra and shut it down! She reeled forward, the cornmeal falling from her nerveless fingers. Only two feet to go! The song continued, welling from some place deep within her. Sweat poured from her body. Chills ravaged her.

Just as the last bit of cornmeal fell from her fingers to complete the circle, Ellie heard a shriek. Stunned by the sound, she fell backward. Instantly, she felt Mac's hands under her arms, steadying her. She gasped for air. Eyes wide, she looked at the darkened corner.

Without a word, she pulled herself from Mac's arms. Steadying herself, she dragged in a deep breath of air. The entity had to flee now that the circle was complete. Shaking badly, Ellie knelt down on the floor and drew out the pipe. She could feel the entity racing around outside the circle. An inhuman screaming began, beating against her ears, against her body. The spirit was shrieking to try to make her lose her focus. Could Mac hear it?

Ellie didn't dare look up to find out. She slid the cedar pipe stem into the red pipestone head, then reached for the tobacco bag. Her hands were sweaty, but she gripped the pipe securely as she stood up and faced the corner where the entity made its home. A terrible trembling moved through Ellie as she took the first pinch of tobacco and faced north within the circle.

"Great White Buffalo," she called out in a strong, clear voice, "please bless us. I ask you to use your endurance and strength to release the spirit over the rainbow bridge." She held the pinch of tobacco high above her head. Her fingers began to warm up and she smiled to herself, feeling positive energy surround her. The blessing of the tobacco had been given and she placed it carefully into the pipe bowl.

Turning, Ellie moved to the east side of the circle. The shrieking continued, buffeting her ears. Their very lives depended upon her fixation on the prayers. She held up a second pinch of tobacco. "Spotted Ea-

gle of the east, I ask your blessing. Please give the
spirit who resides here with us a new beginning, a new
birth over the rainbow bridge.''

As Ellie placed the tobacco into the pipe, she felt a
sudden gust of chilling air. It was real air, not spirit
wind from another dimensional level. She realized
with a start that the entity was now pooling its energy
and literally creating wind. And he was aiming that
wind at the cornmeal circle! Ellie had never seen an
entity so resourceful. She watched as some of the
cornmeal was blown toward them. Would the circle
hold if the cornmeal was removed? She wasn't sure.
This had never happened to her before.

So many things went through her mind, but she put
them aside. Going to the south, Ellie called upon
Grandfather Coyote. The wind continued. More of
the circle was blown away. Were their lives in jeopardy? Could the physical removal of the cornmeal
spell their death? Ellie hurried to the west, the direction of death and rebirth, and Grandmother Medicine Bear. Her prayer said, she lifted the pipe in a
semicircle above her head.

''Father Sky, I pray for the release of the spirit.
Take him into your arms and take him safely across
the rainbow bridge.''

Ellie felt a quivering begin in her solar plexus, her
stomach area. A cold chill struck her in the head. She
anchored her feet, knowing in that moment that the
entity had destroyed their circle of protection. It was
going to attack her, to try to stop her from releasing
him. Every cell in her body tensed, every bone, every
joint and every muscle. The physical attack was dev-

astating to Ellie. She forced herself to complete the semicircle to Mother Earth, and pronounce the appropriate prayer.

As she did so, a hand wrenched at her arm. The pipe was nearly jerked out of her grip. No! If the pipe was taken, it would be smashed, its power destroyed. Fighting the cold working through her, Ellie knelt down, her movements jerky and uncoordinated. With a shaking hand, she found the lighter and grasped it tightly. Once the pipe was lit, the entity would no longer be in charge.

Her breathing grew labored. She felt the choking hold around her throat again, saw her vision graying. She couldn't stand; she didn't have the strength. The entity was sucking the life out of her. She no longer felt her feet or legs. The numbness was spreading quickly. *Hurry! Hurry!* she entreated herself.

Shutting her eyes tightly, she forced herself with her last bit of strength to lift the pipe to her lips and light it. Ellie felt as if her physical body was vibrating apart. There was a war going on within her and outside her.

The instant she took the first puff of sacred smoke into her mouth, she heard the entity shriek. Immediately, Ellie felt it leave her, and she forced herself to her feet. She released the smoke in prayer form to the north, then repeated her actions in each direction. A red-hot energy moved through her, flowing out of her feet and hands, moving rapidly through the hangar. Ellie felt the heat. She was sweating profusely, her body quivering, but she continued to smoke the pipe, saying the prayers for release.

The entity howled. It raced around the hangar, trying to outrun the energy of light and love flowing from and through the pipe. As Ellie aligned herself with that energy, with the pure love flowing out to the spirit, she felt deep compassion for it—even though it had tried to kill her. The pipe continued to emit thick, white smoke into the hangar. It curled, took shapes and moved like clouds on some invisible wind. Ellie knew in that moment that she had triumphed with the help of the Great Spirit. But it had been her heart, her ability to remain in harmony with herself, that would now lovingly release this spirit to a far more gentle environment, another dimension, where it could receive the help it needed.

The screaming rose in volume. Ellie felt the entity back into the corner where it had lived for so long. She opened her eyes and saw the white smoke from the pipe gathering in that corner—fine, delicate veils embracing the walls, the floor. She felt the spirit being pulled out of the hangar, being taken to another dimension. Within seconds, she felt a lightening in the atmosphere. The darkness no longer looked so forbidding, the gloom was not so pervasive. She continued to smoke the pipe and send healing, loving prayers to the entity, to pray for its return to goodness and light.

Finally, the pipe was empty of all tobacco. Ellie felt weak as she slowly lowered it and cradled it in her left arm. For the first time, she dared look across the destroyed circle at Mac. He stood there, his face ashen, his eyes dark and his fists clenched at his sides.

"It's all right now," she quavered. "He's gone. It's done...."

Mac moved forward. Without hesitation, he opened his arms and dragged Ellie against him. "Are you okay?" he rasped, kissing her hair, her temple.

With a little laugh, one more of relief than joy, Ellie nodded. "Yes, I'm going to be fine."

"It attacked you again."

"Yes." She looked up at his harsh features, saw the anger and concern in his eyes. "He's gone, Mac. He'll never come back."

"Good." He held her tightly against him, never wanting to let her go. "I was never so scared, Ellie. I felt that bastard hit you again and again. I felt so helpless. So helpless."

"I know." She eased herself out of his arms. "Let's get out of here. All I want to do is go home, shower and sleep. I'm so tired, Mac."

With a nod, he walked over and brought the suitcase to her. Then he looked around. The hangar felt different. There had been no visible change, but that didn't make him any less certain that the spirit was gone.

"Come on, sweetheart, I'll take you home."

CHAPTER TWELVE

Ellie awoke late the next morning. She stretched, luxuriating in the feel of her muscles moving, her toes and fingers flexing. Mac had brought her home, made sure she was all right and then left. Closing her eyes, she recalled how badly he'd wanted to kiss her—but they'd both been too shaken by the events to do much of anything besides say good-night.

Ellie pushed the covers aside and sat up. It was ten o'clock! She didn't chastise herself for sleeping in—between the psychic attacks and the energy she'd spent, she'd needed a deep, long, healing sleep in order to recoup. She felt good and vital this morning.

Near eleven, the phone rang. Ellie picked it up. "Hello?"

"Ellie, it's Mac. How are you this morning?"

She relaxed against the wall, the phone cradled between her cheek and shoulder. "I'm fine, Major Stanford. Better than you could ever believe."

"Good." She heard the relief in Mac's voice. "How are you?"

"After a nightmare-filled sleep, I guess I'm okay."

"Really?"

"My imagination was running away with me. I kept dreaming you were getting killed by that damned spirit."

"I think you were just replaying all the fears you felt in that circle last night, that's all."

"For sure," Mac grumbled. "Listen, I wanted to let you know that I've got a line on this William Treadwell, the man the entity accused of killing him."

"Oh, yes?"

"The provost marshal found out that Treadwell was an officer at Luke in the mid-eighties. The PM's office contacted him this morning—he lives in Casa Grande, a nearby town. They're sending over an investigator to talk to him. I told them to ask him about Tim Olson. I don't know if anything will come of it or not. But I thought you'd be interested."

Ellie's eyes widened. "I wonder if Treadwell will tell the truth. After everything that's happened, he *must* know something about Tim Olson's AWOL status." She gripped the phone a bit tighter.

"I think you're right, sweetheart. Anyway, the PM is reopening the investigation. It doesn't guarantee that Treadwell will admit to anything. Even if he murdered Tim Olson, we might never know the whole story."

"No," Ellie murmured, loving the sound of Mac's voice when he called her sweetheart. "But at least the spirit of Tim Olson has been released, and I know he's in a far better place."

"I wish you could be here today," Mac said. "I'd swear that the hangar looks lighter, brighter."

"I'm not surprised. When an entity is present, a gray film hangs over the area. You don't realize it until it's gone."

With a chuckle, Mac said, "Well, I have to tell you, everyone seems to be a lot less tense this morning. I've got two of my birds in for maintenance. We're using that corner, and everyone is fine. As a matter of fact, there's been a lot of joking and laughing going on over there, and that's kind of unusual."

Ellie heard the awe in Mac's voice. "On a subconscious level, your crew people must have sensed that entity's presence." She shivered. "If I had to work with it around, sucking up energy, I wouldn't laugh or joke very much, either."

Mac laughed indulgently. "You've made a believer out of me, Ms. O'Gentry."

"Thank you, Major, but I don't try to make believers out of anyone. It's not my job. You believe because you had enough proof, that's all."

"Maybe you're right," Mac said lightly.

"Do you think you could get a few days off?" Ellie blurted out, a little nervous over her bold approach.

"Sure. Why?"

"Well, I'd like to take you to a very special place I go. It's a sacred place, Mac, and I'd like to share it with you."

"I'm game."

"It means hiking," she warned.

"I guess this eagle can take a walk."

Ellie's heart expanded with such love for Mac that the words lodged in her throat for a moment. "You truly are an eagle. Thank you for deigning to walk with us mere humans who are bound to Mother Earth."

"I can probably free up a couple of days. Say, Thursday and Friday?"

"Good."

"Where are you taking us?"

She smiled warmly. "That's a surprise, Major Stanford. Just bring along a knapsack, hiking shoes and a hiking stick. Okay?"

"Okay, sweetheart. But really, all I need is you. You know that?"

Yes, she did, she truly did. Closing her eyes, she said, "Thursday can't come soon enough, Mac."

"I know," he rasped. "Until then, you rest and take it easy. You've earned it."

"Well, what do you think?" Ellie asked as she and Mac stood in the forest of Oak Creek Canyon above Sedona. Mac was dressed in Levi's, hiking boots, a red polo shirt and had a hiking stick in hand. "Is it as beautiful as I described?"

Mac smiled down at Ellie. Two days had been pure hell without her, and he was eager to spend the next four with her. She wore her hair in two long braids, and had a pale pink blouse and jeans on. The sunlight reflected off her hair and he longed to kiss her. "What I'm looking at is beautiful," he confided in a low tone.

Coloring, Ellie laughed. They'd held hands the entire drive up from Phoenix. The kiss he'd given her earlier still lingered on her lips and burned hotly in her memory and heart. "We have another six miles to hike before we can pitch our tent. I don't know about you, but I'm starving already!"

Grinning, Mac picked up his pack. "Then let's get on with it, Ms. O'Gentry." He shouldered it and arranged it in a comfortable position against his back. Ellie took the other pack, which contained most of the food for their four-day hiking trip. The scent of pine was thick and fragrant, the trail wide and dry. Nearby, Oak Creek wound in a meandering fashion along the red sandstone cliffs that had long ago been molded by the water's flow.

The trail was wide, and Mac shortened his stride so that Ellie could keep abreast of him. Her eyes danced with delight, and her mouth was curved softly in a slight smile. He knew she was as happy to be here with him as he was to be with her.

"I think we deserve this," he told her as they walked up a steep incline.

"Oh?"

"We've never really had the time we've needed to be with each other."

"That dinner was pretty nice," Ellie said, meeting his smile, absorbing his happiness.

"It was good," Mac admitted, halting at the top to catch his breath. They were at sixty-five hundred feet; though he was used to flying and taking a lot of g's, this was different. Ellie seemed unaffected by the altitude, but then, as she'd told him earlier, she hiked the west fork of this creek often. He could see why: the place was devoid of tourists. Its peace and quietness reminded him of a cathedral.

Ellie wanted to reach up and kiss Mac's mouth, but held back. First she wanted to get them to the camping site she always chose, and then . . . well, whatever happened, happened. She saw the burning desire in his eyes and felt his need of her. It was a delicious feeling, being loved. The sensation was a new one to her, which made it even more wonderful.

"I have some good news about Treadwell," Mac told her as they started down the incline.

Ellie looked at him. "What did they find out?"

"When the investigator went to talk to him, the man broke down and started crying."

Ellie's mouth dropped open. "Why?"

"Treadwell told the investigator that he'd gotten into a fight with Olson—he didn't say over what—and they got into a shoving match with each other. Treadwell pushed Olson and he fell and hit his head against a desk. I guess it killed him instantly. Anyway, Treadwell owned up to everything. He buried Olson's body out on the desert and let everyone think he had gone AWOL." Mac shook his head. "I guess the poor guy was relieved when the investigator came to him. He had a lot of guilt over it."

"How terrible," Ellie murmured. "For Treadwell *and* Olson. Each of them has suffered."

"For a long time," Mac acknowledged. "Anyway, Treadwell is giving his full statement to the PM's office today."

"What will they do?"

"I don't know. A court-martial. Maybe prison. He's hired an attorney—there will be a trial—so we'll just have to wait and see." Mac gave her a look filled with pride. "If you hadn't given me that information, none of this would have been resolved. I'm pretty impressed with you, lady. You and your talents."

Ellie reached out and caught his hand. It was warm and dry, and his fingers curved around hers in a gentle squeeze. "I've got to believe that Tim Olson will know what has happened. Maybe now, he can truly rest in the spirit world."

"I think Treadwell feels relieved, too, in an odd sort of way."

"Justice is always served," Ellie murmured, walking at his side. "We may not see it or be aware of it happening, but the scales of karma are always balanced out in the end."

"I'll be glad to fill my karma with you," Mac teased.

Ellie laughed, her voice echoing softly through the pine. "That's dharma, Mac—the good things in life that we deserve. Karma is the not-so-good stuff." Her eyes danced with joy. "With you, I think it's all good."

"Well, we're going to find out," Mac warned her with a grin. "We're both going to get exactly what we deserve."

Two hours later, Mac stood on the bank of Oak Creek, marveling at the beauty of Ellie's campsite. The sun was overhead, the light filtered, and the shadows cooled the heat to a palatable temperature. Oak Creek was wide here, a fine, gravel bottom, the water clear, the stones dancing with colors of white, blue, black and red; all washed down through the narrow canyon over aeons. He felt Ellie's presence and turned his head to the left. They had just gotten the tent up, and all the equipment set out.

"How about a swim? I don't know about you, but I'm dusty and sweaty." She smiled.

"Swim?"

"Sure. Don't eagles swim?"

Mac grinned and pulled his polo shirt over his head, hanging it on a nearby tree limb. "I do."

Ellie gazed at Mac's lean, hard body. His large, muscular chest was covered with a mat of fine, black hair. He was so beautiful. Did he realize that? He seemed so unaware of the effect of his maleness on her. As she stood looking up at him, his hair was tousled by the slight breeze, and the sunlight emphasized the good, strong bones of his face. It was time.

"I always swim here," she told him. "Naked."

Mac's brows rose. "I didn't bring a bathing suit, either."

With a shrug, Ellie began to unbutton her blouse. "I know." She gestured to the wide, serene creek. "This has always been a healing place for me, Mac. I wanted to bring you here because it was my way of saying that I was ready to heal from my past."

Mac turned and captured her fingers with his. He smiled down at her, then continued to unbutton her blouse. Beneath it she was wearing a white T-shirt. "You helped me heal from mine, so I think the favor ought to be returned, don't you?" His fingers barely grazed her skin as he eased the blouse from her shoulders. He placed the garment next to his shirt on the tree limb.

Ellie nodded. "I was so afraid you'd be like my ex-husband, Mac."

"But I'm not him," he whispered, settling his hands on her upper arms.

"I know that now."

"I didn't blame you, Ellie. We all have wounds. Some of them take longer to heal than others, that's all."

With a sigh, Ellie began to unbutton her jeans. "I just couldn't believe a man like you existed, Mac. I was afraid to...."

He sat down on a smooth, red, sandstone rock. "I know you were." He unlaced his hiking boots, then placed them, along with his thick white socks, on the creek bank. Across the creek rose a five-hundred-foot red sandstone wall, curved elegantly, the rock smooth and undulating. The red of the rock, the dappled clear water of the creek and Ellie's soft voice were perfect for him.

If she was shy about undressing before him, she didn't show it as she slipped out of her jeans and took off her T-shirt. She wore no bra, and he stared in appreciation at her full figure, her curved breasts, her less-than-thin waist and ample, rounded hips. She matched the beauty of the smooth sandstone cliffs across the creek.

With a slight smile hovering around her lips, Ellie tested the water with her toe. "Umm, it's nice and warm." She moved quickly into the creek and halfway across, slid into the depths and disappeared.

Mac watched, mesmerized by the naturalness of Ellie in her surroundings. Her hair was like a floating ebony banner behind her as she swam in lazy strokes, the dusky color of her skin complementing the dappled, sunlit water and rock. Divesting himself of the last of his clothes, he moved into the creek. The water was warm and beckoning, and he waded into the depths of the creek to join Ellie.

The water embraced him like a long-lost lover as he left the gravel shallows and began to swim toward Ellie. Towering pine trees stood on the banks, the breeze touching the tops of them. Somewhere a robin sang a melodic song as Mac struck out in long, sure strokes. The water was refreshing, a welcome change from the hot, dry heat. He felt the sweat and dust wash away, as if hands were skimming his entire body. It was a luxurious feeling, and Mac laughed out loud. He hadn't skinny-dipped since he was a boy.

Ellie grinned as Mac lunged for her. She dove, escaping him. The water was clear and she could see where she was swimming. The red, pink and white gravel shimmered below her as she kicked strongly toward the red sandstone cliff. She twisted and turned, sometimes feeling his hand grasp her ankle, but always managing to free herself. With a laugh, she surfaced. Mac had probably *let* her escape!

Joyfully, Ellie turned just as he swam up to her. His hair was slick and plastered against his skull; water dripped down his smiling face. This wasn't the air force pilot, or the eagle. This was the man she loved with an intensity that frightened her. He treaded water and opened his arms to her. When she swam to him, the pleasant shock of their warm bodies meeting made her gasp. Mac's arm moved around her waist and he drew her hard against him.

His mouth crushed hers in a wet, cool kiss that rapidly heated up. Ellie surrendered to his strength, to his hunger, and eagerly returned his molten kiss. She was wildly aware of his male length against her, sliding, touching and caressing her here and there. Finally, breaking the kiss, Mac swam with her to a more shallow area. Standing on the gravel bottom, he slid his arms around her shoulders.

"Now you're caught," he growled, and triumphantly claimed her full, waiting mouth. Ellie tasted like hot sunlight, sweet, fragrant pine and cool mountain water as his fingers tunneled through her wet, sleek hair. He tipped her head back just slightly, drowning in her lushness. This woman was part magic, part earth and all his. He would never get enough of her. As he lightly grazed the full crescent of her breast, he felt her tremble.

Without a word, Mac eased his mouth from her lips, smiled into her brown eyes shining with desire and picked her up. He had spotted a grassy bank that had escaped the dense shadow of the pine trees. It had just enough room for two people. The water dripped off him as he made his way to the bank and stepped up into the thick, soft grass. As he laid Ellie down, he marveled again at her natural beauty. Nothing had ever seemed so very right to Mac as this moment out of time with her. She placed her arms around his shoulders as he settled beside her, propped up on his elbow.

Ellie sighed as Mac's mouth once again ravished her, teased her and promised so much to come. Her fingers sought out his broad chest, tangled in the wet curls, and she felt the thunderous beat of his heart against her palms. As his hand drifted down the side of her neck, he kissed her more deeply, the heat bubbling wildly between them. His fingers followed the crescent of her breast, and she moaned, wanting more, wanting him. Their bodies were still wet, still slick from the water, the grass a counterpoint in texture beneath her back. It was soft, tickling and giving.

The taste of Mac, his maleness, filled her senses as he kissed her hungrily, taking, giving and then taking again. A fiery rhythm ignited between them, her breath matching his own, the frantic need of her body matching his. He tightly gripped her shoulders, pulling her upward to meet him.

A cry of pleasure tore from Ellie's lips as he sank swiftly, deeply, into her. The white-hot heat of sunlight had met and been encased in the cool, moist depths of her like the coolness of the water beside them. A shudder of pleasure rippled through her as he took her, established a wild, hungry rhythm born out of primal need and swept her off into a world of light, color and senses.

The ripple of the creek, the song of the robin, the whispering breeze through the pines and his hard, warm body taking her all conspired with her spinning, enriched senses. The texture of Mac's taut skin, his masculine scent, the pressure of his mouth against hers competed with the sounds surrounding her. Each thrust, each movement heated her flesh, made it tingle, and created an awakening ache within her. She started to cry out like a wolf with her lifetime mate.

Sunlight danced with the breeze. Their breath mingled, moistened, became frantic and punctuated. Each powerful movement ignited a new sense of rising fulfillment deep within her. The eagle and the earth had met and now were one in a union of earth and sky. A cry began to tremble through Ellie as their bodies fused in that one, molten moment. It was a cry of such utter pleasure that all she could do was arch deeply into Mac's arms, press herself against him and give herself to him in an act of surrender that brought tears to her closed eyes.

With a groan, Mac managed to keep most of his weight off Ellie. He felt her breasts touching his chest, her moist breath riffling against his cheek, and he smiled. He felt incredibly drained; it was as if someone had literally taken him apart and put him back together again. He lay weakly above her, drowning in the splendor of her fragrance, the warmth of her body and the sigh of her uneven breathing. He watched her flushed face, saw how pouty her lips had become in the aftermath of his hungry kisses. He knew he'd given her pleasure; they had shared themselves on a level he'd never before this moment realized existed.

Gently, Mac eased to one side. As Ellie's lashes fluttered open, he was struck again by the golden beauty of her brown eyes. How beautiful Ellie was, how much a part of Mother Earth she was. He smiled. He was a part of the earth now, too, in a special and important way. Words were useless as he stared into Ellie's smiling eyes. Mac felt such a living, breathing connection between them that he was in awe. Lightly, he skimmed her dry shoulder, caressed her breasts and allowed his hand to move downward, outlining her full hip.

"I think this eagle just got grounded."

With a rippling laugh, Ellie placed her arm on his shoulder. How natural it was to feel this kind of intimacy with Mac. "No one cut your wings."

"No." Mac chuckled and leaned down, capturing her lips one more time. As he pulled his mouth away, he looked intently into her eyes. "You know, you're like wine, Ellie. Sweet, fragrant wine. I can't get enough of you, your taste, the feel of you." He ran his hand gently across her flank.

Closing her eyes, Ellie smiled, satiated. "Me? I can't stop touching you, kissing you...." And she couldn't. How long they lay there on that sun-dappled bank, with the green grass beneath them, the earth cradling them and the creek singing, Ellie didn't know. Their kisses were long, exploring, sweet and tender. With each caress, she absorbed the strength of him, and returned it to him with her own womanly strength.

Finally, as the sun began to dip behind the pines, they stirred out of each other's arms. Mac got up and claimed their clothes. They dressed lazily. There was no hurry, just a sense of intimacy he never wanted to let go of. After Ellie slipped into a pair of moccasins she'd brought along, she came over to where he sat lacing up his hiking boots. She crouched down behind him, placed her arms around his torso and rested her head against his back.

"I love you," she said.

Mac froze momentarily. He turned in one motion and brought Ellie between his thighs. She knelt before him, her hair loose, thick and dry.

"I've loved you from the start, sweetheart," he told her. "I just didn't realize it until about two weeks ago." He placed a small kiss on her nose and watched her reaction. Ellie's eyes widened with surprise, and then filled with tears. How easily she was touched! "A little while ago, Ellie, when I had you in my arms, I realized that this is what I'd been waiting for all my life. I was always unfulfilled, even though I'd achieved success as a fighter jock. Johanna couldn't stop that hunger in me." He kissed Ellie's brow and eased back enough to hold her luminous gaze. "It's gone, Ellie. I feel like a man who was given back his life, his dreams, with you in my arms. It might sound corny, but that's how I feel."

She shook her head and caressed his stubbled cheek. "No, it's how I feel, too. As we made love with each other, I realized how Mother Earth was loved by Father Sky. I understood, for the first time," she whispered in awe.

Mac nodded. "Chemistry might disagree with you about air and earth being compatible elements, but for us, they are."

"And I was so afraid to admit to myself, much less you, that I had fallen in love with you, Mac. It just happened. I never expected it. I had given up on ever loving again, when you walked into my life."

Wryly, he said, "Makes two of us, sweetheart. We both made mistakes, or at least poor choices."

"You were wounded, but at least you had the courage to try again," Ellie said, her voice strained. "I was too scared."

Laughing, Mac said, "And here's the lady who will go up against a malevolent spirit that could kill her before she blinked an eye." He gave her a small shake. "You don't know your own courage, Ellie, but I do, and that's all that counts."

She stared with wonder up into his smiling eyes. How lucky she was to have found this man, who accepted her fully—just the way she was. She was not a beauty, didn't have a model's body and had one of the most unusual life-styles a person could have. But he relished it—and her. He loved her without apology, and without conditions. Moving into his arms, Ellie framed his darkly tanned, lean face with her hands.

"I'll love you forever, Mac. Forever...."

EPILOGUE

If Mac had ever had any doubts about Ellie, her way
of life, or what had made her the unique woman he
loved, they were laid to rest now. He stood out on the
porch of a small house with a tin roof, a cup of freshly
made coffee in hand. He was on the Qualla Reservation, home of Ellie's mother, Walks With Wolves, and
her younger sister, Diana. The late summer fra-
grances, some from a profusion of wildflowers that
surrounded the house deep in the *hollar,* or meadow,
embraced his nostrils.

Taking his other hand out of his pocket, he moved
to an old, well-worn porch swing and sat down. Inside the house, he could hear Ellie's husky laughter
combine with the rest of her family's. They'd arrived
two days ago, and after being wooed by the beauty of
the Great Smoky Mountains of Cherokee, North
Carolina, Mac didn't ever want to go back to his base
in Phoenix. The swing creaked softly and he pushed
it slowly back and forth with his weight.

The hollar was surrounded by huge, rounded
mountains that stretched as far as he could see. Deep
in the woods, a blue jay that had been startled shrieked
over the intrusion. Mac saw a black crow winging its
way silently across the light blue of the early morning

sky. He sipped the coffee carefully, savoring the flavor of the blend.

This morning, he and Ellie were going to be married—by Walks With Wolves. The intervening months had been like a dream come true for Mac, and he could think of no finer way to honor Ellie and her Native American way of life than to be married at her childhood home on the Qualla Reservation. He watched as the veils of silent fog twisted and moved through the thick woods. That was why they were called the Smoky Mountains, because fog was a constant part of this region.

"You look dreamy," Ellie observed, coming to a halt at the screen door.

Mac roused himself from his reverie and gazed up at Ellie. His mouth curved ruefully. Gesturing for her to come sit with him, he murmured, "I've come to the conclusion that this place is magical."

Smiling, Ellie opened the screen door. She wore a simple yellow cotton skirt, a flowering print blouse, and her hair was in two thick black braids. As usual, Ellie was barefoot as she walked across the aged wood of the porch and joined Mac on the swing.

Entwining her hand with his, she said, "I loved growing up here. We had the woods, the animals and insects as our teachers."

"No crowded cities, pollution or noise," he murmured grimly, lifting her hand and kissing the back of it.

Her skin tingled pleasantly as she held his warm gaze. "Now you can begin to understand why I am the way I am." With a grin, she stuck out her bare feet, which were thickly callused on the soles. "I never wore shoes as a kid. Mama had to *force* me into wearing them. I hated them. I felt fettered, like a wild horse who had to wear a saddle it hated."

Mac placed his arm around her shoulders and drew her closer to him. "I think that's what I love about you most—your sense of freedom, your unapologetic individuality."

Laughing, Ellie pressed a kiss to his recently shaven cheek. How handsome Mac looked in the gray slacks and white silk shirt, open at the collar to reveal a tuft of his dark hair. She sobered and nuzzled his cheek while holding his tender gaze. "It means everything, darling, that you're here with me."

He saw the rest of the unsaid statement in her eyes. Ellie had been married to her ex-husband by her mother, and he'd turned around and insisted a *real* reverend from a recognized church perform the ceremony all over again. Mac wasn't going to insist on that at all. "Well," he whispered, capturing her hand with his, "I wanted things perfect—for both of us."

Tears glimmered in Ellie's eyes and she laughed and wiped them away. "Sometimes, Mac, I think *you're* a dream. You're magical to me, you know."

He sat back, contentment washing through him as never before as they swung gently back and forth. "Me? The last three months have been a special hell, if you ask me. I haven't felt very magical." With the IG out of the way and with Mac's squadron getting top honors, life had finally settled down—a little. Things never settled down much in the military, however, and his time with Ellie was always shorter than he wanted.

"You're magical to me because you honor me for what I am and am not." She glanced up at his serene features, that face she knew so well, loved so much. "When you asked me to marry you, I never dreamed you'd want Mama to marry us. That means so much to me, Mac. I know my way of life and my beliefs are different from yours, but you have this ability to transcend our differences and make it work." She shook her head in amazement. "That's why you're magical to me, darling."

He caressed her shoulder. In a few minutes, Ellie would go back into the house and dress in her Cherokee finery for the wedding. "My last marriage taught me a lot," he told her gravely. "I tried to make Johanna fit into my vision of what she should be in the marriage, and she rebelled. She was right to divorce me. I learned my lesson, Ellie. I'm finding that our differences don't have to put us at odds with each other—they teach me new things and I like that. I just hope I bring as much wonder, awe and discovery to you from me."

Smiling, Ellie said, "You do, Mac. You always will."

"It's time!" Diana called excitedly from the screen door. "Come on, Ellie. Mama's got your buckskin dress ready!"

Ellie smiled up at her younger sister, who had already dressed in her ceremonial finery: a gold-colored deerskin dress with beads adorning the neck and sleeves. She gave Mac a quick kiss.

"Are you sure?"

He held her serious, dark eyes. Cupping her cheeks, he said, "I've never been more sure of anything in my life, Ellie. Go get dressed. . . ."

Ellie rose and moved quickly to the screen door that her younger sister held open for her. Diana resembled their mother in that she was shorter and more curvaceous than Ellie, who had taken after her father in the height department. But of course Ellie still had her mother's wonderful, rounded figure.

Diana giggled and grabbed her by the arm as they moved through the kitchen. "Wait until you see the dress Mama made for you. Oh, Ellie," she sighed. "It's *beautiful!*"

Mac smiled and heard the women giggling as they went out of earshot. From down the winding, narrow dusty road he saw a number of cars beginning to arrive. In less than half an hour, Walks With Wolves would perform the sunrise wedding ceremony. His heart beat a little faster, but it was with love for Ellie, and a yearning to make her his wife for the rest of his life.

The cars, at least two dozen of them, slowed to a halt near the white picket fence and border of bright red geraniums. The wedding guests—Cherokee friends of Ellie, some of whom she'd grown up with, and others, relatives of their large family—began to emerge. Mac stood up and went to the edge of the porch. He marveled at their laughter, the light dancing in their eyes and their colorful finery. Huge drums were carefully taken out of the trunks of three cars, and set beneath the spreading arms of a huge cotton-

wood that was at least two hundred years old. The
drums were set on special tripods, about a foot off the
ground.

Cherokee women, some dressed in modern instead
of ceremonial clothes, came carrying dishes for the
potluck that would be held afterward. The odors of
fried bacon and ham tickled his nostrils. The many
children frolicked like happy, unfettered puppies. Mac
saw at least another dozen cars coming down the road.
He grinned. Walks With Wolves was a greatly loved
medicine woman on Qualla, and Ellie had warned him
that probably half of the reservation would come to
help them celebrate. The Cherokee loved any kind of
ceremony. And what could be more joyful and sacred
than a wedding?

The older Cherokee women, most of them with steel
gray hair, were clearly the leaders of this celebration.
Mac realized he was seeing a matriarchal culture at
work, and it worked without dissension. The amount
of food being taken into the small kitchen was overwhelming! Ellie had told him that Joe Thunder, an
elder, had barbecued a quarter of a deer especially for
the wedding celebration. Mac thought it must be more
than that when it took three stout young men to carry
the armloads of the foil-wrapped meat into the
kitchen.

Mac saw a young woman wearing a beige-colored
buckskin dress begin to play a flute. She was in her
teens, but she was beautiful. Mac shook his head as he
tried to absorb all the busy activity, the smiling men
who came over to shake his hand and congratulate
him, and the nonstop laughter that filled the air. Now,

he understood why Ellie missed her people, the reservation. It was a way of life. A better way in many respects.

The drummers began to beat the elk-hide drums, which were each at least twenty feet in diameter. They were deep-throated drums, and Mac wondered if Ellie would go into an altered state upon hearing them. He smiled a little. She wouldn't, of course, because if she felt half as excited as he did, she'd be firmly rooted in the here and now—with him.

The drumming became louder, more resonant, filling the hollow, and the laughter lessened and the children gathered solemnly around the three drummers and their huge instruments. The spreading arms of the cottonwood were so large that they would easily shade everyone—and there had to be at least two hundred people, from what Mac could estimate. There was a new excitement in the air, and he could feel it. He ached to see Ellie, to share these discoveries with her. Mac didn't feel like an outsider. Instead, everyone was making him feel a part of the tribe. It was a humbling feeling.

Diana was the first to emerge from the house. She grinned and took him by the arm. "Come on, I have to lead you down to where the drummers are sitting."

"Is everything okay?"

"Sure. Wait until you see Ellie. She has never looked prettier."

The Cherokee friends and family parted as Mac and Diana made their way toward the drummers. A table had been erected in front of the drummers. There was a brightly woven cloth over it, and Mac saw a beaded

eagle-feather fan with dark red and white fringe
hanging down like a tassel from the end of it. He also
noted a piece of black pottery and recognized the sacred sage that had been ceremonially wrapped. There
was a stalk of freshly cut corn on the table, too.

"Stand here," Diana said, and pulled him to a halt.
"You can face toward the house. Mama and Ellie will
be coming in a few minutes." She smiled happily and
took a large armful of sage from one of the older
women. Thanking her, Diana held out some to Mac.
"Here, hold this sprig of sage throughout the ceremony." Diana turned and began giving each partici-
pant a piece of the cut sage.

The drumming softened, and an old, slightly
hunched woman who looked to be in her eighties came
forward. Thin as a bird, her face pinched with age, her
eyes were fiercely proud and snapping with life and
light. She wore a red skirt, white blouse, and red shawl
and a necklace of polished agate around her neck. Her
thin, white hair was braided with red ribbons. She had
a cane, and she hobbled to where Mac was standing.
Mac nodded deferentially to the elder, for the old
people were greatly respected and well cared for on this
reservation. He watched as she slowly straightened her
curved back and threw back her shoulders. That aged
face, carved with wrinkles of life, began to glow as she
lifted her chin and opened her mouth to sing.

The sound that came out of the woman's throat
astounded Mac. The old woman's voice was like that
of a clear, alto bell. He was amazed by the clarity, the
strength of it, as she sang a song in Cherokee. The
crowd was quiet, respectful, as the song grew in vol-

ume, in beauty, and the entire hollow filled with her joy.

Mac felt his heart opening, like a flower, as the old woman sang several songs in a row. He had no idea what they meant, but it didn't matter. The feeling was all that counted, and this woman, who sang from her heart, left no one untouched by the powerful emotion of her voice. There were tears in nearly everyone's eyes—including his own.

Just as the last song ended, the drums picked up the beat, sounding like rhythmic thunder. Mac looked toward the porch. His heart lurched, and he held his breath for a moment. Ellie was dressed in a white deerskin dress. Her black hair was still braided, but now fluffy white eagle feathers adorned the end of each braid. The sunlight, just peeking above the mountains, glinted off her hair, giving it blue highlights, making the purity of the dress even more dramatic, if possible.

The white deerskin dress had colorful beaded work across the neck, down the shoulders and around the bottom of it. Fringe, thick and long, hung at least two feet from the end of each sleeve, and moved like wheat being lulled by the wind around her feet. Ellie wore white deerskin boots trimmed with intricate beaded designs. They were knee-high, and small brass hawk bells and a colorful array of glass beads hung from the fringe that encircled the tops of them.

With each step, the faint tinkle of the hawk bells could be heard. Ellie carried a large, dark brown wing of a golden eagle between her hands. The bottom of it was wrapped in bright red leather, fully beaded, with

red and white fringe hanging at least two feet below it.
She wore large abalone disc earrings, with small, fluffy
white eagle feathers suspended from each one by colorful red leather. In her hair she wore two large brown
feathers with white spots near the base, the leather and
beads curving across her skull and hanging over her
left ear.

Mac felt dizzied by the picture Ellie presented. She
was no longer a modern-day woman, but a Cherokee
shamaness of immense power and unrivaled beauty.
With each step she took, made in time with the sonorous beat of the drums, the fringe of the dress moved.
She looked as if she was floating, not walking on solid
earth. Everything moved with her, in unison, and Mac
began to understand what Ellie meant by being in
harmony with one's self and with everything else.

She wore no makeup. The flush of her cheeks, the
radiant golden glow of her skin, combined with her
dark, velvet-brown eyes made her look incredibly
beautiful to Mac. Their eyes met. His heart almost
burst with such a fierce feeling of love, he couldn't
breathe momentarily. Ellie's gaze was shy, the light in
her eyes gold with hope, shining with love for him.

He was so stunned, so riveted on Ellie, on her slow
movement toward him, that he barely realized that
Walks With Wolves proudly followed behind her
daughter. She, too, wore a beautiful buckskin ceremonial dress, only it was gold colored, and far sim-
pler in design. No, Ellie was the center of attention,
and Mac smiled to himself. Her mother had worked
for years on this special ceremonial dress, after Ellie's
divorce. Because Walks With Wolves was clairvoy-

ant, she could often see into the future for a person.
She'd told Ellie that this time, when her wedding dress
was worn, it would be forever. Never had Mac wanted
anything more than to have Ellie as his wife—forever.

Walks With Wolves, large and rotund, moved with
a flowing grace as the drums continued their respectful beat. She raised the wing of an eagle high into the
air, and a chorus of old women standing to the left of
the drummers began. Their voices rose high, war-
bling, and echoed throughout the hollar. Then a chorus of men, who stood on the other side of the
drummers, began to sing. The song was joyful, vibrating and blanketing the entire assembly.

Mac automatically reached out as Ellie drew near.
She shifted the eagle wing to her left hand and reached
for his. He couldn't stop smiling or looking into her
dark, soft eyes. For an instant, he didn't feel of this
life, but of another. He wasn't a pilot, but an Indian
warrior, and this was the woman he was going to wed.
That déjà vu passed quickly as Ellie's fingers tightened around his and they turned toward the altar,
where Walks With Wolves had taken her place behind
it.

The thundering drums began resonating more
quickly. Walks With Wolves lit the sacred, ceremonially gathered sage, the white plumes of fragrant smoke
leaping into the air. She smudged herself with the
smoke by using the eagle-feather fan on the table.
Then, coming around the altar, she smudged Mac and
Ellie, both front and back, with the sacred smoke. Finally she walked in a slow, sunward circle, the sage
lifted high. The breeze was playful, and everyone

watched as the smoke moved first to the east, then to the south, to the west, and finally to the north.

Walks With Wolves grinned and nodded. That was a good sign. She went back behind her altar and placed the sage in the black pottery bowl, the smoke continuing to purl and twist into almost animal or human forms. The song ended, and the drumming halted.

"Osiyo," she greeted everyone, "it is a good day to die. It is a good day to live." Her eyes sparkled as she looked around the assemblage. Picking up the eagle-feather fan, she pointed toward the couple. "Sunrise means the beginning of all things. Father Sun rises in the east to give us his light so that we may live. Let Mac Stanford walk forth this day with my daughter, Iya, Pumpkin, hand in hand. Heart with heart."

Smiling, she turned and faced the east, the feather raised above her head. "Awohali, eagle of the east, we ask your blessing upon this couple that stands before you. The man is of eagle parentage, like you, Awohali. Bless him with the insight into Iya's heart and soul. Let him always realize that as he must fly free, so must she. Bless their union with one another." She turned back to Mac and Ellie. "You face the east because this is the point where all things begin, good or bad. It is the point of birth and rebirth."

She turned to the south, the feather raised in that direction. "Grandfather Coyote, we pray to you to bless this couple that stands before you. Give them the hearts of children, give them laughter and the humor to laugh at themselves. Let them both realize that pride and ego are unwanted in marriage." She turned to them. "The south energy is about growing, about being a child. Too many adults lose their ability to laugh. You will cry together. Be sure to laugh together, too."

Mac felt a lump in his throat as Walks With Wolves turned to the west, the direction that lay directly behind them. He gently squeezed Ellie's fingers and saw, as she lifted her chin to look at him, that she was crying. In that moment, all he wanted to do was wrap his arms around her and hold her forever.

"Grandmother Medicine Bear," Walks With Wolves intoned, "I ask you to bless this couple that stands before you. Grandmother, you are about dying, and I ask that you help this couple to release anything that would hurt their love for one another, to let it die a natural death between them. Take whatever bad memories or wounds that still might linger in their hearts and dissolve them with your healing power." She turned to them. "The west is about death and transformation. A good marriage goes through many ups and downs, but through it all, the man and woman must agree to let some things die between them that no longer serve in a positive manner to their marriage. If they do this, then there is always room for new growth. The west is about continued growth throughout life. Let the seeds planted in the east grow in the south and come to maturity in the west."

Ellie sniffed and self-consciously released Mac's hand to wipe her eyes. Diana leaned over and pressed a white linen handkerchief into her sister's hands. Ellie smiled weakly and dabbed her eyes. Clenching the handkerchief, she felt Mac's dry, warm hand enclose hers once again.

"Great White Buffalo," Walks With Wolves called, facing north. "We ask you to bless this couple that stands before you. Give them the wisdom of their years, the wisdom and clarity of their experiences to guide them through the trials that await them." She looked at them gravely. "The north always reminds us of our responsibility to others, to our family, and to all our relations. It is the point of clarity, common sense and practicality. It is where all your experiences go to become maturity, and then, ageless wisdom. The north tells us that the seed of your love, planted in the east, growing rapidly in the south and coming to fruition in the west, will be harvested in the north."

Walks With Wolves moved around the table once more and pressed the brown and white feathers of the eagle fan against Mac's chest. "May his heart—" and she moved the feathers to Ellie's breast "—and her heart become one. May they beat with the same rhythm of love." She touched Mac's brow and Ellie's brow with the feathers. "May their thoughts be of their love and respect for one another." She touched Mac's heart and Ellie's abdomen. "May their love bring children who will be greatly loved into this world."

She put the fan on the altar and picked up the large ear of ripe corn. Placing the corn between them, she asked them each to place one hand upon it. "Corn is sacred to us. It is about fertility, about life, about food and surviving. She is always female, always woman, and it is the Great Spirit who blesses the Cherokee people with such fertile abundance. I pray that this abundance is passed on to each of you, to your hearts, to your children to make you strong for one another."

Ellie took the ear of corn.

"I believe you have a ring to give her, eh?" Walks With Wolves said in a sweet, beguiling voice, her smile large with expectation.

Mac nodded, and gulped. He was on the verge of tears, something quite rare for him. He fumbled for and finally found the ring in his pocket. It wasn't an ordinary kind of wedding ring. Mac had gone to a jeweler who had found an exquisite tourmaline gemstone that had the rainbow colors of pink, green and blue in it. Ellie had told him many times about the rainbow bridge, that passage that stood like a vast, beautiful opening between earth and heaven. In her work as a shamaness, she had helped many people over that bridge. The symbology was beautiful, and Mac had had a ring fashioned out of gold to hold the square-cut, highly faceted gem.

Ellie was his rainbow. His joy. His pot of gold.

Walks With Wolves eyed Mac pointedly as Mac took Ellie's finger to slip the ring on it. "You had something to say, maybe?"

"Oh . . . yes . . ." Mac grinned a little, embarrassed. The ceremony, the singing and drums, had been overwhelming to his senses, and he'd nearly forgotten that he'd asked Walks With Wolves for a moment to say something personal to Ellie as he placed the ring on her finger. Mac felt the heat rise in his cheeks, and he saw Ellie smiling tenderly up at him.

Clearing his throat, he rasped, "This ring symbolizes how I feel about you, Ellie. The pink is about my love for you, the green about growth that we'll share between us." He smiled. "Maybe the growth of a baby or two..."

There were sighs and expressions of agreement all around them, and Mac saw tears of joy come to Ellie's eyes. "And—" he gulped "—the blue is the sky that I fly in, which has become a second love compared to the love I feel for you." He slipped the ring on her finger and then whispered, "I'll love you forever...."

Tears spilled down her cheeks and Ellie heard the collective sigh of all the women around them as she lifted her arms and placed them around Mac's neck. He held her tightly, his face buried against her hair. "And I love you, too," she said softly, leaning back just enough to kiss him on the mouth.

His mouth captured hers in a swift, hot, indelible kiss that seared her heart and burned into her soul. The drums began a hard, startling fast beat. Both male and female singers sang. All Ellie was aware of was Mac's strong arms about her, holding her tightly against him, and his worshiping mouth taking hers, giving back to her, in those golden moments of time.

Dizzily, she felt Mac release her just enough to allow her to put her feet back on the ground. Walks With Wolves grinned broadly, her cheeks flushed, her eyes wet with tears. Without a word, Ellie put her arms around her mother, held her, thanked her. The people began to dance in a large circle about the altar, swaying, moving and singing. They linked hands, their feet shuffling softly in the green grass, their voices lifted up in unison and joy.

Diana hugged Ellie and then smiled through her tears. Ellie whispered her thanks to her sister and gave her the eagle wing and the sacred corn. Taking Mac's hand, Ellie led him to the circle and the people allowed them in. Mac didn't know the dance step, but he tried, and after a moment, caught on to the simple toe to heel movement.

Mac had eyes only for Ellie, for the way she swayed with the drumbeat, with the thundering sound echoing and reechoing throughout the hollar. Her brown eyes sparkled with tears and love. Her mouth, soft from his branding kiss, made him ache to take her away from here and make hot, melting love with her. Mac knew that would have to wait until at least sundown, when the marriage feast would end. For the rest of the day, there would be a tournament of horseshoes which he was expected to take part in, one of the Cherokee's favorite games. There would also be softball, volleyball and other competitive sports, followed by feasting, more singing and more dancing. He didn't mind because through it all, Ellie would be at his side.

When the sun sank behind the Great Smoky Mountains, and the shadows of the night moved silently across Father Sky, they would leave for a cabin deep in the Qualla Boundary Reservation—a special cabin owned by Ellie's parents. It was an old cabin Ellie's hardworking father had built before she was born. As the children arrived, he'd built a newer and larger home in the hollar. Mac had seen the old, wooden cabin, and was eager to be up there with Ellie in the embrace of thick woods and the meandering stream that flowed beside it. There was an old, creaky brass bed that had a brand-new quilt on it, a wedding gift worked on throughout the summer by the women elders of the tribe. Mac was stunned by the outpouring of gifts and generosity from the Cherokee.

As he fell into the slow dance step, with the circle of people moving in a clockwise order with the drumming, Mac laughed. The sound was drowned out by the whoops, the yells and warbles of the people. Ellie laughed with him. He gripped her hand solidly in his. She was his wife! Finally. Forever...

*   *   *   *   *

Watch for LOVERS DARK AND DANGEROUS, *the Silhouette Shadows 1994 Short Story Collection due out in October. It will contain a mesmerizing story by Lindsay McKenna featuring Diana's romance!*

SILHOUETTE® *Shadows*™

Welcome To The
Dark Side Of Love...

AVAILABLE THIS MONTH

#27 HANGAR 13—Lindsay McKenna
Mac Stanford didn't believe in the supernatural, yet what else could explain the eerie events in Hangar 13? To compound matters, he had to enlist the help of shamaness Ellie O'Gentry. She challenged his view of reality, while his powerful attraction rocked her safe world. And all the while, the menacing spirit in Hangar 13 grew ever more deadly....

#28 THE WILLOW FILE—Lori Herter
When Arianne Lacey encountered the darkly handsome stranger on the beach, she couldn't know the fateful history they shared, nor the fated attraction. Ross Briarcliff's great-grandfather had allegedly killed Arianne's great-great-aunt, Willow, pitting the families against one another for all time. Ross was determined to solve the legend surrounding her ancestor's death—a legend that seemed very much alive in Arianne....

COMING NEXT MONTH

#29 LOVER IN THE SHADOWS—Lindsay Longford
Molly Harris teetered between the brink of madness and imminent murder charges. Three episodes of amnesia had coincided with three killings, making her doubt her innocence, as did enigmatic detective John Harlan. Harlan's logic told him she was the one, but the shadowy cover of night offered him different answers—and a dangerous attraction. To save Molly's life, Harlan faced the ultimate test—exposing his dark side....

#30 TWILIGHT MEMORIES—Maggie Shayne
Wings in the Night
Rhiannon and Roland de Courtemanche had roamed the earth several lifetimes over, but until the present they had only their private pains to heal and only their immortal souls to protect.... Hunted like animals by a relentless pursuer, they strove to save the life of a child, and to ensure their endless love for all eternity.

Take 4 bestselling love stories FREE

Plus get a FREE surprise gift!

Special Limited-time Offer

Mail to Silhouette Reader Service™

3010 Walden Avenue
P.O. Box 1867
Buffalo, N.Y. 14269-1867

YES! Please send me 4 free Silhouette Shadows™ novels and my free surprise gift. Then send me 4 brand-new novels every other month, which I will receive months before they appear in bookstores. Bill me at the low price of $2.96 each plus applicable sales tax, if any.* That's the complete price and—compared to the cover prices of $3.50 each—quite a bargain! I understand that accepting the books and gift places me under no obligation ever to buy any books. I can always return a shipment and cancel at any time. Even if I never buy another book from Silhouette, the 4 free books and the surprise gift are mine to keep forever.

215 BPA AKZH

Name	(PLEASE PRINT)	
Address		Apt. No.
City	State	Zip

MEN OF COURAGE
by
Lindsay McKenna

It's a special breed of men who defy death and fight for right!
Salute their bravery while sharing their lives and loves!

Be sure to catch this exciting new series, where you'll meet
three incredible heroes:

Captain Craig Taggart in SHADOWS AND LIGHT (SE #878),
available in April.

Captain Dan Ramsey in DANGEROUS ALLIANCE (SE #884), May.

Sergeant Joe Donnally in COUNTDOWN (SE #890), June.

These are courageous men you'll love and tender stories you'll
cherish…only from Silhouette Special Edition!

As seen on TV!
Free Gift Offer

With a Free Gift proof-of-purchase from any Silhouette® book, you can receive a beautiful cubic zirconia pendant.

This gorgeous marquise-shaped stone is a genuine cubic zirconia—accented by an 18" gold tone necklace.

(Approximate retail value $19.95)

Send for yours today…
compliments of 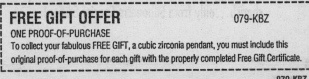 *Silhouette*®

To receive your free gift, a cubic zirconia pendant, send us one original proof-of-purchase, photocopies not accepted, from the back of any Silhouette Romance™, Silhouette Desire®, Silhouette Special Edition®, Silhouette Intimate Moments® or Silhouette Shadows™ title for January, February or March 1994 at your favorite retail outlet, together with the Free Gift Certificate, plus a check or money order for $2.50 (do not send cash) to cover postage and handling, payable to Silhouette Free Gift Offer. We will send you the specified gift. Allow 6 to 8 weeks for delivery. Offer good until March 31st, 1994 or while quantities last. Offer valid in the U.S. and Canada only.

Free Gift Certificate

Name: _____

Address: _____

City: _____ State/Province: _____ Zip/Postal Code: _____

Mail this certificate, one proof-of-purchase and a check or money order for postage and handling to: SILHOUETTE FREE GIFT OFFER 1994. In the U.S.: 3010 Walden Avenue, P.O. Box 9057, Buffalo NY 14269-9057. In Canada: P.O. Box 622, Fort Erie, Ontario L2Z 5X3

FREE GIFT OFFER
079-KBZ

ONE PROOF-OF-PURCHASE

To collect your fabulous FREE GIFT, a cubic zirconia pendant, you must include this original proof-of-purchase for each gift with the properly completed Free Gift Certificate.

079-KBZ